A NEW ♥ HEART

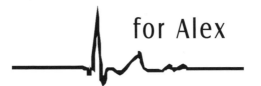

for Alex

A NEW ♥ HEART

for Alex

Manak Sood, M.D.

Rutledge Books, Inc.   Danbury, CT

ALL RIGHTS RESERVED
Rutledge Books, Inc.
107 Mill Plain Road, Danbury, CT 06811
1-800-278-8533
www.rutledgebooks.com

Manufactured in the United States of America

Cataloging in Publication Data
Sood, M.D., Manak

A New Heart For Alex

ISBN: 1-58244-212-6

1. Medicine

Library of Congress Catalog Card Number: 2002106952

Dedicated to
my wife Lucienne and three beautiful
children, Anjali, Surina and Evan.

Special thanks to
my parents, Sheila and Sagar,
for all their help

CHAPTER 1

He could feel himself awakening and it was obvious the operation was a success. A distant conversation was barely audible and appeared to be between a doctor and nurse. The inability to open his eyes and move his extremities became increasingly alarming as consciousness was regained.

An overwhelming sensation of being choked overcame him, as the endotracheal tube remained lodged deep within his throat. Alex could not find a means by which to communicate his fears, and resigned himself to becoming a spectator in his own hospital room. There was no doubt about it; he was dependent on the ventilator and on the medications infused into each arm. He continued to listen to the surrounding dialogue.

"We've maximized the blood pressure medications, Doctor Addison, but his heart just isn't responding. What's next?"

"I'm not sure, but I'm pretty worried about him. The post-operative echocardiogram looked like crap! I think he took a huge hit coming off bypass. Have we tried pacing him?"

"You bet, and it hurt us bad. His pressure dropped like a rock and his oxygenation became progressively worse. He looks pretty broken to me."

The nurse was stating the obvious and Dr. Addison glanced wryly in her direction. "Oh no, he's sagging again. Bring the code cart around and gather the team. I'll begin chest compressions."

Alex remained in a semi-lucid state as his cardiac surgeon commenced chest thrusts. He felt no pain, but the pressure with each heave was unbearable. Drugs were rapidly administered in each arm by the resuscitation team but proved ineffective. He could slowly feel himself rising above the bed. This afforded him an unprecedented view of the efforts below. His drifting continued and eventually he was hovering over the hospital, being drawn toward an incandescent light in the distance. The light became progressively brighter until . .

Alex awoke from his sleep as the sun shone through the window. It cast an eerie shadow as it slipped through the vertical blinds and illuminated the wall opposite his bed. He sat up and was acutely aware of the stillness in his home. Sunday mornings were typically quiet in the Harkins' household and Alex was predictably the first one to rise. He did not find the silence disturbing but rather used the time productively to

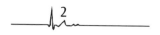

reflect on the previous week's developments and chores for upcoming days.

After rubbing the sleep from his eyes, he panned the room spending a few moments reflecting on his possessions. A nightstand was located adjacent to his bed and held an alarm clock, CD player, and the fourth edition in the Harry Potter series. Alex had taken to reading avidly over the last two years as his heart condition had left him progressively incapacitated. This activity required minimal exertion and had become both an outlet and escape as his illness progressed.

He kept several automobile magazines in the uppermost drawer. He'd been a car buff all of his life and couldn't wait to purchase his first Porsche. He had convinced himself that this acquisition would confer him instant celebrity status in his small hometown and had taken this vision one step further in his mind. At the bottom of the drawer, Alex kept a list of individuals who would be offered rides in his sports car and this roster was as dynamic as the weather, depending on who was considered a "friend" at the time.

Alex's dresser was located in a corner of the room and housed several baseball trophies. There were three in total and each contained a golden athlete poised in the batting position mounted atop a plastic stand. The inscriptions read, "Mills Creek Gophers-League Champs" and were dated between 1997-1999. He was not particularly talented when it came to sports and had become progressively limited in his exercise tolerance over the last two years. Fortunately, there were no formal tryouts for the Gophers and Alex was allowed to play despite his lack of ability and stamina. He was aware of the team's generosity regarding this matter, and made up in team spirit what he lacked in physical attributes. Although unable to take the field during games, he regularly attended practices and emphatically stated that once his heart was fixed, he'd be competing for the starting shortstop position.

In another corner of the bedroom were a beanbag chair and a chess table whose pieces remained in position from last night's match with his father. An artist in India carved the pieces from sandalwood and the set was a gift to Alex from his uncle after a journey to the Far East. Each man remained pleasantly aromatic despite stiff competition from the laundry hamper in the closet. The table itself was cast in alternating squares of green and white marble inlay with a rosewood border.

Alex's passion for chess was second only to reading and both activities required, as a common denominator, minimal exertion. He knew that although his chess-playing prowess would never afford him a varsity letter or help him to win over a girl, this activity would remain with him into adulthood. As his oxygenation declined, he was drawn to these sedentary pursuits and excelled in them accordingly. Unlike other children, he didn't think of accomplishments as being determined on a field or court but rather had resigned himself to accepting the limitations of his condition and making the most of every day. In this way, he was precociously mature for a child of eleven years.

The walls in Alex's room were covered with the requisite posters of sports stars and teen idols save one watercolor hanging over his bed. This composition had been left for him by his maternal grandmother and depicted a young child who was ill and surrounded by angels. The coloration of painting and the angels enamored Alex in particular. Their bluish hue had a transcendent quality that proved to be reassuring as he became progressively discolored from a lack of oxygen. The painting instilled in him calmness and provided a personal guarantee that as his illness progressed, he would be looked after by angels. This serenity was readily apparent in the eyes of the child depicted on the wall and helped him not to fear sickness or death.

Alex quietly got dressed and scampered past the other bedrooms and down the stairs. His two sisters shared a bedroom adjacent to his, the nursery for his baby brother was next, and his parents' master bedroom was at the end of the hall. The circular staircase connecting the upstairs and downstairs was laden with family portraits. He assumed this descent in a deliberate manner, as always, taking time to inspect the familial timeline represented by the pictures. With each step he saw his sisters grow older as documented by their school photographs. They looked so healthy and had changed exponentially over the years.

As he continued his descent, Alex paused in front of a black-and-white photograph of his grandparents on their wedding day. He loved the pictures for reasons that were unclear to him. It was perhaps the essential lack of color that was appealing; all those depicted in the portrait appeared a ghostly white. Over the penultimate step was a portrait of Evan. He, too, was diagnosed with a heart ailment although the doctors had reassured his parents that no surgical intervention would be needed. How lucky, Alex thought.

The stairway led to the family room, which was connected to the kitchen via an arched doorway. Alex continued his morning ritual quietly as the rest of the family remained asleep. This routine included raiding the refrigerator for any item that could be construed as breakfast food which, at his age, included pizza and leftover meatloaf. He chased these breakfast delicacies with a healthy portion of fortified milk.

The kitchen drawer under the computer contained his cardiac medications and he began the lengthy process of their consumption. This activity, in itself, was relatively time consuming given the obligatory pauses between swallows. He was convinced that the tablets, given their size, were originally meant for horses, and had only recently been approved by the FDA for human consumption. The litany of medications he was required to take may have proven intimidating for a lesser soul, but this practice had become commonplace, and almost integral, to his morning routine.

Between pills he glanced at the magnetic calendar fastened to the refrigerator door. This invaluable resource served as "command central" at the Harkins' household and effectively coupled parental resources with children's events. This synchrony was paramount in a family with four children.

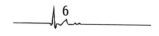

Much to his chagrin, and unlike most months, there was a paucity of activities involving his siblings and he had all but monopolized the upcoming week. The events read as follows:

Monday: Alex says goodbye to friends and empties school locker

Tuesday: Northeast flight 248 leaves Mills Creek 8:00 A.M. Arrives at Hitchcock 10:30 A.M.

Wednesday: 8:00 A.M. appointment with Dr. French

Ridgewood Children's Hospital
11:00 A.M. heart catheterization
6:00 P.M. Dad arrives flight 131

Thursday: Surgery at 11:30 A.M.

Friday was blank, but it was the day Alex cared about the most. Would he be awake? Would the breathing tube still be in place? Would his heart be working well, or at all? A myriad of unanswerable questions ran through his head at a dizzying pace and he decided to get some fresh air. He had been waiting for this day impatiently for the last two years and as it approached, a group of butterflies had taken residence within his stomach next to the meatloaf and pizza.

His favorite sweatshirt, embroidered with the Miami

Dolphins logo, hung lazily on the coat rack by the screen-door exit. He hurriedly slipped it over his head as he stumbled past the enclosed porch into the backyard. Mills Creek was located on the southern coast of Maine and the Harkins' home backed up to Almond Bay as it fed into the Atlantic Ocean.

As always, the view was magnificent. The backyard was a narrow strip of grass which was separated from the cool Atlantic waters by a four-foot sand dune running the length of the property. From atop the dune, an unobstructed view of the bay, incoming ships, and Maine's rocky coastline was afforded. Alex had seen this panorama for years, yet each time the landscape remained impressive.

He panned the shore and his eyes set upon McGinty's Pub. This gathering place had been a staple of the community since the early 1800s and continued to flourish as sea trawlers and their inhabitants routinely docked at its pier. Not infrequently, Alex had heard from his bedroom the drunken drawl of returning sailors as they exited the eatery. He had mastered the profanities of various dialects just by keeping his ear to the window.

There was no Mr. McGinty nor, as rumor had it, had there ever been. Folklore stated that a fisherman's wife had opened her home to other wives as they waited for their husbands to return home during the heyday of the industry. With time, it had gone public as fishing was replaced by tourism and remained a right of pilgrimage for local teenagers as they approached the drinking age. Anecdotally, Alex heard that an initiation process involving the eating of live eel and swimming in the frigid coastal waters awaited the youngster ready to enter adulthood, although these rumors had never formally been substantiated.

Growing up, he had stared at the establishment for hours on end and had formulated a detailed mental picture of its layout. He envisioned a square-shaped wooden bar with inscriptions dating back a hundred years; over the generations, sailors from various foreign ports had frequented McGinty's and Alex was sure they had etched highlights from their travels on the bar surface. The walls, he imagined, were covered with fishing nets, anchors, foreign flags, and portraits of revered captains from the past. These adornments most likely covered the entire surface of the wood paneled room and also the loft, which harbored a long table reserved for weary sailors resigned to eating and drinking the night away. He expected the fare to be poorly cooked but devoured handily, without complaint, by the patrons who were grateful for having any warm, home-cooked meal. Alex could not wait to visit the pub on his twenty-first birthday and confirm his vision of its interior.

He continued to scan the bay as its eccentricities provided an excellent distraction from thoughts of his operation. His eyes eventually came to rest on a large colonial house three doors from his own. This was the home of Sandra Cromwell, Alex's second, but most significant, crush. The Cromwells were an affluent family who had recently relocated from Portland. Sandy's father was the head of a large pharmaceutical company and bonded with Alex as he, too, had had open-heart surgery.

Despite the fact they were the same age, Sandy clearly had twenty pounds and four inches on Alex. This discrepancy was partly due to the inherent variance in growth trends between adolescent males and females, but also resulted from the malnutrition resulting from his chronic illness.

Sandy was dark haired with stunning blue eyes. Occasionally, as they played, he would feel a little "weak in the knees" when she made direct eye contact and although this phenomenon wasn't completely clear to him, he didn't think it was worth the effort to figure it out. Of all his friends, Sandy was clearly the most supportive during the perioperative period, having lived through the process with her father. His fondness for her had grown significantly in the last few months. In fact, her support gained her the pole position on Alex's list of potential candidates for Porsche rides.

The sun continued to rise, as did the temperature, and Alex removed his sweatshirt, wrapping it around his hips, as he headed home for breakfast. This stretch of the beach was somewhat rocky with jagged boulders between the dunes and the ocean, with smaller pebbles scattered among the hard sand approaching the shoreline. Seaweed was strewn perpendicular to the sea as it was left behind by the outgoing tide.

The brief walk had proven therapeutic, and as he approached his home, he saw the Cromwells heading in the direction of town. Alex and his father would visit Main Street later that morning, a Sunday ritual, and he hoped to see Sandy at that time.

He paused before entering his home and peeked through the back window. The entire family was now awake and situated around the kitchen table awaiting breakfast. His father sat at the head of the table and was flanked by his two daughters. Mark Harkins was a cardiac surgeon at Mills Creek Community Hospital and although he limited his practice to adults, he was quite informed regarding the potential complications and pitfalls surrounding Alex's operation and the stress was obvious in his demeanor. Alex's oldest sister Annie sat in the next chair. She was seventeen years old and had recently begun the college application process. Annie was beautiful with long black hair, a dark complexion, and stunning brown eyes; everyone thought she resembled the Pocahontas character in the Disney movies. Annie stood first in her class in academics and played varsity tennis and gymnastics in the winter. He couldn't have asked for a better big sister, he thought.

In the next seat was Molly, his fourteen-year-old sibling. She was small in stature but equally beautiful. Molly was somewhat of a tomboy in her attire and recreational pursuits. Still an underclassman, she was on the girl's varsity basketball team and was voted to the state's all-star team two years in a row. Molly had pampered Alex as long as he could remember, and the two had remained intimately close through her adolescence. In fact, she confided things to him in the last few years that positively could not have been discussed with parents. Most recently, she had received detention for truancy and although she had skipped school many times in the past, this was the first time she had been caught. On prior occasions, she had forged her parents' signature on absentee excuses and had become quite proficient in reproducing her mother's handwriting. Alex thought that this was an excellent attribute for any child during the school years and he hoped he could benefit from her talents when his time came.

On Molly's last attempt, however, she had been seen at the mall by one of the nuns from school and this incrimination was inarguable. The penalty was relatively benign for her "first" offense and consisted of remaining after school on three consecutive days bearing the wrath of Sister Agatha's piercing stare. Her attempt to submit a note stating she could not remain for detention for family reasons resulted in her downfall as an alert nun questioned its legitimacy and phoned home. Unfortunately, Molly's cover was blown and her forgery ring earned her two more weeks with the good sister. Relentless, Molly informed Alex that her next out-of-school adventure was rapidly approaching and extended him an invitation to accompany her. He had politely declined as his palms were still reddened from Sister Agatha's last disciplinary action with a wooden ruler.

Alex gazed across the room at the seat directly across from his father. Jane Harkins was a nurse by trade but had stopped working after Molly's birth. Her experience, coincidentally, included three years in a pediatric intensive care unit in Portland. This background gave her unfortunate insight into her son's upcoming procedure and her anxiety became palpable as the surgery approached.

She was a pretty woman with a dainty figure, which she inexplicably kept hidden under old sweatshirts and baggy pants. Her hair was as gray as it was black and her blue eyes were not passed down to any of the children. Next to her was little Evan. Alex stared at him intently and thought he was the cutest baby he'd ever seen. He was particularly proud of Evan's healthy, cherub-like cheeks. Evan looked so healthy and alive he could have adorned any vegetable jar in the Gerber food labels, in Alex's opinion.

The empty chair next to Evan's was his own. A chill went down his spine, as the scene was reminiscent of the Dickens classic, A Christmas Carol, with Alex representing the Tiny Tim character. He visualized what life would be like if he were no longer there and could feel the tears welling up in his eyes. It was obvious that life would go on in his absence. This moment of self-pity was interrupted as abruptly as it began when a piece of toast entered his peripheral vision as it headed directly for his head. He was sent reeling backward for several steps as the food missile slammed against the window. He scanned the room in efforts to identify the culprit and saw his father burying his head, hiding a smile. Alex correctly identified the source of the projectile. Mark Harkins was quite pleased with his aim.

"Come on in, Alex! It's time to sing 'Happy Birthday' to your mother."

He reentered the kitchen sheepishly, lest another grain product be hurled in his direction, and tossed his sweatshirt across the room. It landed like a horseshoe on the appropriate hook on the coat rack and he muttered, "Sure, lucky in horseshoes . . . "

"Good morning, Mom, and happy birthday!" He leaned over and kissed her forehead.

"Are you trying to make a break for it before your surgery, son? You're certainly up and about early this morning."

"If I were going to make a break for it," he replied sarcastically, "I'd grab Dad's car keys and would be halfway to Mexico by now!"

"I don't think little blue Americans are in demand in Mexico," his father chastised, "and if you touch my car keys I'll take a sliderule to your palms instead of a ruler. Sister Agatha would be proud of me! By the way, that was a nice game of chess last night, son, but tonight I'm going to kick your butt!"

He winked at his father knowingly, as he hadn't lost a match to him in years. Alex had noticed that each time his father looked in his direction recently, he would become teary eyed and melancholy. Part of this was obviously related to the surgery but it went deeper than that; he had overheard a conversation between his parents in which his dad had become quite emotional. His father had devoted much of his life to becoming a heart surgeon and felt he hadn't been there for his family when needed.

"If I could do it all over again," Alex had overheard his father say, "I would have picked a different profession and concentrated on being a better father. Now our boy is having a major operation and we may lose him. How can I possibly make up for lost time?"

"Don't worry, dear. You've always been there for this family, whether you realize it or not." His mother offered these conciliatory words sincerely but his father was inconsolable. This was the first time Alex had heard his father cry.

"Well, where are my birthday cards?" the conversation continued. The children went to their bedrooms and returned with their offerings. Molly's was handed over first and was a Hallmark special purchased from the town's drugstore.

"That's lovely, sweetheart."

Annie's card was next and was clearly a homemade greeting. Its cover was adorned with hearts shaded in by Crayola crayon. The words "I Love You Mom" were spaced across the top of the construction paper and were barely legible.

"Gee whiz, Annie, who helped you write this card, Evan?"

"Funny, Mom. It's the thought that counts." The thought

earned Annie a kiss on the forehead.

Finally, it was Alex's turn. His card was also on construction paper, but much more artistic than Annie's. This time, his mother laughed out loud.

"All right, what's so funny?" Annie asked, suspecting she was on the receiving end of the joke.

"I was just thinking about the natural evolution of birthday cards, Annie. It seems when children are really young, they have no money and have to make the greeting cards themselves. Somewhere in early adolescence cards are bought from allowances or money earned from working. This phenomenon comes full circle, however, when children are in their late teens and homemade cards seem to make a comeback, usually at the last minute! Forgot my birthday again, Annie?"

The entire family broke out in laughter as his sister turned as red as her nightgown. After reading Alex's card, Jane became extremely emotional and excused herself from the room.

"You know what, guys? There's been altogether too much crying and hugging going on around here lately, and I'm getting a little tired of everyone feeling sorry for me. It's just a stupid operation. It's just a big cut over my breastbone. It just requires that they stop my heart for a couple of hours. Okay, so there'll be some blood loss . . . " Alex's attempts at calming his mother lost credibility as his dissertation continued. His speech became more deliberate with each uttered phrase and he assumed a distant gaze. It was obvious he was petrified! Unfortunately, this exchange resulted in more tears and hugs.

"Enough of this girly stuff already!" his dad barked. "Let's wolf down some grub before we head into town."

The girls and the baby stayed behind while the men rode into Mills Creek. Dr. Harkins mounted his ten-speed after pulling the moped from the garage. Alex had found cycling to be increasingly difficult with his low oxygen saturations, prompting his father to purchase a motorized cycle for his ninth birthday. He peddled until he became short of breath and converted to the motor as needed.

"C'mon, son! Keep up if you can!" his father yelled as he raced out of the driveway onto Wildflower Drive. Alex followed immediately and had caught up before turning onto the road heading toward town. He was visibly short on oxygen and his face and nail beds turned a light shade of blue.

Alex reverted to the motor as he continued down scenic Route 7. This race had become a ritual between the pair but Dr. Harkins had an ulterior motive in challenging his son; as Alex's condition worsened, his lack of oxygen became more obvious at progressively shorter distances from home. The earlier he had to stop, the sicker he was getting. Dr. Harkins used this marker as a gauge to aid the timing of surgery.

The road into town hugged the coastline and the entire ride was less than three miles. It was a beautiful trip. Now that the motor was on, Alex could enjoy the scenery. He remained on the designated bike path and, given the flawless weather conditions, was joined by numerous cyclists with the same idea. A steep and rocky cliff separated the road from the shoreline and at the halfway mark was a jagged, rocky prominence that resembled the Sphinx in Egypt. Coastal winds had transformed the amorphous cliff into one of the undisclosed natural wonders of the world.

At its irregular base was a grotto that had been carved out by the ocean's tides over thousands of years. The entrance remained the size of a garage door and could easily accommodate a small craft; Alex and his father had taken their sailboat into the grotto the previous summer. It was magnificent inside and had a greenish hue as the sunlight reflected off the water onto the rocks. They had carved their names into the edifice using a Swiss Army knife. Alex loved knowing that his name was buried in the cliff forever and this feeling of immortality proved reassuring as the week was unfolding.

The two made a right turn off of Route 7 at the ESSO gas station onto Main Street. Mills Creek was a prototypical New England town situated between the Allegheny Mountains and the Atlantic Ocean. Main Street itself was out of a Norman Rockwell painting and the locals joked that it could serve as a Hollywood set, if needed. At the north end of the thoroughfare was St. Theresa's church with its pointed steeple, which could be seen from miles around.

The two parked their bikes on the other end of the roadway. The first stop was always Zinger's Deli.

"Mornin' gents," Mr. Zinger shouted enthusiastically as he reached for two beverages behind the counter. "A black coffee for the good doctor and an orange juice for the town's next great heart surgeon, Alex."

The drinks were on the counter before the two visitors could say hello. Dr. Harkins had always joked that coming to Zinger's was like visiting the pub on the television show "Cheers"-a friendly place where everyone knows your name was the show's motto. Zinger's appeared as if it came straight out of New York City; in fact, Mr. Zinger had spent his entire life in Brooklyn and had only moved to Mills Creek within the last five years. He maintained that within the confines of the store, he felt as if he were at home.

The windows were partially covered by large tubes of meat suspended from the ceiling. A glass display the width of the store housed cheeses from all over the world arranged in various settings depending on the approaching holiday. The corner pantry housed fresh breads and pastries. A fan located directly overhead funneled the room's aroma onto the street under the store's canopy. According to Mr. Zinger, this was an old Parisian trick to lure passersby into the boulangeries and bakeries. He contested, "If it's good enough for Frenchy, then it's good enough for me."

Normally the pair would purchase luncheon meats and bread for the upcoming week, but since they would be spending it at Ridgewood's Children's Hospital, it seemed pointless. Mr. Zinger never let them pay for drinks and this occasion was no different.

"Good-bye!" Alex yelled as they were leaving.

"Au reservoir and Guten riddens," Mr. Zinger replied mocking the French and German salutations, respectively. Alex shut the door behind them and had a final sniff before moving on.

Two brick sidewalks lined the street. Paired lampposts formed an arch covering the boulevard with the lights nearly touching in the midline. Green ivy crept up the lamps' bases and wooden benches were located after every third fixture. Large, rectangular planters housing trees were set back slightly from the road and served as convenient seating during the summer months. Several small cafés would have outdoor seating, weather permitting, and the tables sat under large, colorful umbrellas.

Stoplights were mounted at street corners instead of hanging overhead and were contained within antique brass boxes. During the Christmas holidays, large banners traversed the thoroughfare at each intersection and the trees were engulfed in lights. This gave the town the appearance of a glass globe one could shake to give a snow effect. The roadway itself between the deli and the church was paved with brick giving it a quaint, colonial look.

As their next stop, Alex and his father visited McKinley's Country Store, which was located between the bank and Zinger's Deli. Entering this establishment gave the feeling of walking into a store from the Wild West of the 1800s as the building's interior had changed little over the last century. The floorboards were originals; wide wooden planks ran the length of the store and creaked with each step. Gunpowder and oil lamp stains gave the floor a weathered appearance.

Suspended from the ceiling by fine cords were lightbulbs without shades, which swung to and fro each time the door opened. The scent of leather permeated the interior, reminiscent of a rural barn. Alex was particularly fascinated by the bear pelts and mounted animals, which lined the windowless walls, akin to a hall of fame for slain animals.

Alex thought Mr. McKinley was quite a character and he had become one of his favorite townsfolk over the years. The store owner was reminiscent of Dickens' Scrooge with his lanky appearance and fine gray hair, a band of which was strapped across the dome of his head connecting small islands of fuzz over each ear. Alex thought this resembled a man wearing headphones and wondered why anyone would consider such a lame attempt to cover baldness.

Mr. McKinley's nose had a crooked tip, which, in profile, resembled the front end of a Concorde airplane. The underlying chin was pencil-like in its pointiness giving his face a triangular appearance. The overall effect was that of a jagged, aged, and callous man, but Mr. McKinley actually harbored the largest heart in Mills Creek.

"Good morning, fellas!" McKinley screamed across the room as Alex and his father entered the store. "You couldn't ask for a more beautiful day. Big week coming up, son?" He knew about Alex's heart condition and upcoming surgery and couldn't have been more supportive. "It's nothin', this open heart stuff, son. Heck, I bet it's trickier to lance a hemorrhoid. Right, doc?"

Mark Harkins offered a weak and nervous laugh while nodding in the affirmative.

"You know, Alex, my wife had bypass surgery and lived for twenty more years, God rest her soul," McKinley continued. With this utterance his voice cracked and his eyes filled with tears as they always did when he reminisced about his wife. "Those newfangled toys these young heart surgeons are playing with these days make surgery seem like one big video game. Right, doc?"

"You bet, Ian," his father replied. "In fact, I think I'm going to open a cardiac surgery arcade for all the kids."

Alex loved wandering through the country store, especially the second floor that contained a small toy department; the closest major toy store was forty miles away in Beaverton. Mr. McKinley was emphatic that his toys were wholesome and low on technology like the ones he had as a child. There were no video games or superhero comics in this repository. Endless wooden bins filled with jelly animals, yo-yos, toy soldiers, wooden cars, and dollhouse furniture occupied its loft.

Typically, Alex purchased one item on any given Sunday, but since he was going away, and his father thought the more distractions the better, he was allowed to choose several items. Instinctively, he chose a travel chess game, some books, and a rubber band propelled airplane constructed from balsa wood that he would fly in the hallways of the hospital. His father chose several chocolate bars for the duo and they met at the cash register.

"Oh, wait!" Mr. McKinley shouted, "I have a small package for you! Please don't open it until the night before your operation." He gave Alex a small gift in red wrapping paper and he placed it with his other purchases.

Alex said an emotional thank you and good-bye as he exited the store. Beyond the town hall and post office was the Mills Creek pharmacy. This facility was quite modern and, implicitly, incongruous with the rest of the town's architecture. Given his medication requirements, Alex was considered a VIP and his father had joked that he alone funded the building's addition completed the previous year.

"Our favorite frequent flyer!" Mrs. Arneson greeted as the pair entered her store. She was a widow who had inherited the business after her husband's untimely demise and although she never took much interest in the pharmacy until his death, she found the daily workings to be an excellent distraction from her empty house.

"Heck, Mrs. Arneson," Alex replied, "with all my medication bills I should be able to fly back and forth to China three times over." She agreed and joined him in a chuckle.

Mrs. Arneson was a pleasant lady in her mid-fifties. She was slightly plump and had the cheeks of a cherub; this latter quality reminded him of baby Evan. Her attire was right off the Broadway stage with sequins, lace, and bright colors; again, quite out of place in conservative Mills Creek. The Arneson family had donated quite a bit of money to the town over the years and had single-handedly financed the town's park. For this, Alex felt indebted.

She pulled up his account on the computer and informed him that he shouldn't need refills at this time. He stated that he was not here for that reason but rather to pick up several periodicals for the upcoming week.

"That's right! This is the week, isn't it?" She winked at him willfully as if she knew everything would be all right. Alex didn't particularly care for the store's interior and much preferred the quaintness of the McKinley franchise. As he approached the magazine rack, he noticed the cover of Road and Vehicle magazine. The sight of the new Porsche twin-turbo made his heart race. He thought it funny that the only times he was aware of his accelerated heart rate was in the presence of Sandy Cromwell and while reading about cars; obvious parallels were drawn.

He chose this issue and a monthly chess periodical. He placed the latter publication under his arm, lest he be seen with it by one of his friends and, thereby, confirm his super geek status. As he was walking toward the counter to pay, another magazine caught his attention. A model in a bikini straddling a toy horse graced the cover of Horn Dog Magazine, and he couldn't help but pause despite realizing that he was in jeopardy of being reprimanded if caught.

Alex sheepishly picked up the magazine and began fingering through it when his father approached from behind and placed a hand on his shoulder.

"Put that down and come out with your hands up, you little pervert! Jesus Christ, son, eleven years old and already a bag of hormones. Could you at least wait until you are a teenager, you miniature Peeping Tom!" His father was laughing inside but had to maintain a sense of decorum in efforts to save credibility.

Alex shook briefly from being startled and in one move replaced the magazine and headed toward the checkout counter. "That's better," his father said as he began to flip through the periodical himself. Alex caught this out of the corner of his eye and laughed to himself.

As Dr. Harkins was paying, the Cromwells entered the

pharmacy. Alex had hoped to see them while in town and, once again, became acutely aware of his racing heart. "There he is," yelled Mr. Cromwell, "the man of the hour!"

He was a tall gentleman, like many corporate executives, who was also bald but made no efforts to conceal it. His rounded head was mounted on a relatively thin frame giving him the appearance of a giant lollipop.

"Gonna get you one of these, Alex?" he said while unzipping his sweatshirt and displaying the scar from his recent bypass surgery. "Don't worry, the girls will love it. You can make up some crazy story about a war injury or knife fight you participated in if they're curious."

Alex remained speechless. Although he realized Mr. Cromwell was trying to be humorous, this dose of reality was overwhelming.

"Hi, there," Sandy spoke, breaking the trance.

"Oh, hi Sandy; I was hoping to see you here," he admitted somewhat uncomfortably. After some persuasion, he convinced Sandy to join him at the park. The couple broke off from the adults and headed toward St. Theresa's Church and adjacent playground.

"Are you nervous?"

"Just a little bit, Sandy," he replied trying to maintain a

manly composure. The remainder of the walk to the north end of Main Street was spent in silence as Alex became preoccupied with thoughts of the surgery and Sandy respected his privacy.

The church was an intimidating brick structure with heavy, paired bronze and wooden doors giving the overall impression of a medieval castle. The spiked steeple was barely visible from the entrance steps. It housed a large bell, which chimed on the hour. There was no dysmorphic caretaker living within its confines as a bell ringer, but rather a Swiss mechanism made it as accurate as Big Ben in London. The townsfolk set their watches by it without reservation as it struck twelve times each day at noon. The Arnesons had also paid for its restoration.

Behind the church was a playground containing two slides, a swing set, a sandbox, and a fort constructed of wood interconnected by suspended monkey bars. This play area was a town project and Alex had participated in its construction during healthier times. He felt quite proud of his contributions although it reminded him of his current limitations. At the base of the fort was a wooden plank on which all the individuals responsible for its existence had engraved their names. Alex considered this his second attempt at immortality.

Beyond the playground was a wire fence enclosing the basketball and tennis courts. He could see the silhouettes of two children in the distance as they played hoops. As he and Sandy approached the group, he could clearly identify the players; it was a two-on-two game and on one team were Eddy Marks and Joey Narato, his classmates and close friends.

Eddy was the son of a banker and excelled at basketball. He was invariably chosen as the first player during pickup games. Joey was a smallish child, not unlike Alex, and suffered from profound hearing loss. They hadn't been close until recently. The reason for this newfound friendship was multifactorial but was primarily a result of Alex's declining health. The sicker he became, the less he could participate in school activities, especially if they involved physical exertion. In a way, he and Joey were both considered disabled; not in the purest sense of the word, but by their exclusion from the normal activities of childhood. He acknowledged the two had formed a strong bond. This phenomenon was not completely unanticipated, as most individuals in the minority seem to band together.

Joey required bilateral hearing aides and because his family was not affluent, he was limited in choice of apparatus; the inexpensive hearing aids were large plastic devices which wrapped around the ear with a small projection placed directly within the canal. From behind, Joey looked like he was wearing earmuffs. This appearance earned him many undesirable nicknames such as "Dumbo," "antenna head," "cauliflower," and "plastic man." Alex remained impressed by Joey's coping skills as he regularly shrugged off these derogatory comments without incident. He felt he could learn a lot from his hearing-impaired friend.

The other team consisted of Barney Freeborn and Zeke Morrell. This pairing was a classic case of good vs. evil as these two were clearly the most rambunctious and intimidating boys in the fifth grade. Both were products of underprivileged homes and what they lacked in money, they made up for in meanness. Alex thought it ironic that the nastiest children he had encountered were always the biggest. He had become a strong proponent of Darwin's theory of survival of the fittest.

Barney was a large, uncoordinated, brute of a child whom everyone assumed had been held back in school for several years (although this was not true). He believed that basketball was a full contact sport and that other children yelled "foul" with careless disregard when on the opposing team. Barney was usually shirtless with denim overalls and torn sneakers like some Pickwickian reject from a Mark Twain novel.

Zeke Morell was as tall as he was fat, which made him essentially round. His standard attire consisted of an untucked, oversized, and stained T-shirt with gym shorts. Predictably, Zeke would be seen with shoelaces dangling several steps behind him, which led to the hypothesis that he couldn't see over his belly to address the problem. Alex thought someone like him might benefit from loafers so this would not be an issue. So one team had speed and intelligence and the other brute strength and ignorance.

"Hey look, it's Alex and Sandy!" Zeke shouted.

"Yeah, what do you know," chimed Barney, "we could

certainly turn this into a three-on-three game. What do you think, little rich boy?"

This remark was obviously directed at Alex and he declined politely. He was petrified of playing basketball in front of Sandy as this would invariably result in embarrassment. His heart raced and his palms became sweaty as he hoped that the conversation would be dropped.

"Come on, what are you a baby, Ritchie Rich?"

Alex's worst fear was realized. The conversation would not be dropped; in fact, it became more inflammatory. He refused again, this time fearing physical retribution.

"Okay, you two," Barney continued, "four-on-two. That's my final offer!"

"Let's do it, Alex," Sandy whispered. "I hate these jerks, always have. Let's stick it to him." She began strolling toward the court and Alex realized he was committed to join her or suffer the consequences from the Neanderthals across from him. He convinced himself that if he maintained a slow pace and used cunning instead of strength, he'd be fine. Stepping on the court, he realized what a huge mistake he had made and the thought of Sandy watching as he became ill made his stomach turn. Against his better judgment, and purely motivated by Sandy's request, he acquiesced. The game began innocently as the "good guys" drove down the court for an uncontested layup.

"Nice shot, cauliflower head!" Barney shouted at Joey.

The game became more physical as the bullies leveraged for several unanswered points. The obvious standout for Alex's team was Eddy and the monsters decided to key on him. Alex fed him an inbounds pass and Zeke and Barney converged and slammed into him from both directions like a double hipcheck. The ball fell out of bounds and Eddy fell to the floor. His wrist was smashed and if it hadn't been for the proximity of the two brutes and fear of their teasing, he would have burst out crying. Instead, he clenched his teeth and called, "Foul."

"The hand's part of the ball," was the ever-intelligent retort from Zeke. "So are the head, the body and legs!" he continued. Adding insult to injury, the unsightly gladiators gave each other a high-five in clear view of the opposing team.

Apologetically, Eddy asked his teammates if he could be seated as his wrist and forearm became progressively swollen. They all agreed reluctantly. Sandy gave the next inbounds pass to Joey, who motioned Alex to advance down the court. He obliged, once again against his better judgment, and began a full sprint toward the opposite basket. Ten yards into his fast break he could feel his heart racing. The initial palpitation became a full-fledged pounding as he posted himself under the backboard.

Alex watched as the ball was hurled in his direction. His

vision became blurry and his head light as Zeke descended upon him. His visual changes digressed into a tunnel vision and only vague shapes were discernible. The ball hit him in the chest and sent him reeling backward, but this was the least of his problems.

His shortness of breath became progressively worse as the oxygen in his blood was shunted through the hole in his heart, bypassing the lungs, and out to the body. He became visibly discolored. Alex initially turned a shade of blue and this discoloration was followed by a more worrisome gray. He became clearly disoriented as the oxygen debt worsened. Feeling faint, objects around him seemed to move with a tail as if he were having a hallucination. He could clearly distinguish Sandy's silhouette and although her mouth was moving purposefully, the words seemed jumbled and incomprehensible. His shorts became moistened as he lost bladder control. Sandy screamed for assistance.

Meanwhile, not missing an opportunity, Zeke and Barney began a barrage of insults. "What's the matter? Did you see a ghost, Alex?"

"Look, he's turning into Casper! I hope he's friendly."

"It's really not that cold out here, Alex! Want a jacket?" Those bastards didn't miss a beat before initiating the insults.

Fortunately, Alex's father was watching the game from the church steps and came running. He knew exactly what was happening. Alex was having a "spell." In other words, he was critically low on oxygen. There was no time to lose. After giving a reassuring wink to Sandy, who by now was cradling Alex in her arms preventing his head from contacting the asphalt, Dr. Harkins immediately loosened his son's shirt and began talking to him using a forceful tone.

"Alex, stay with me, son. You've got to listen to me right now!" Mark Harkins grabbed his son by the shoulders and tried to rouse him. Alex came to enough to cooperate, but was clearly disoriented.

"I'm with you, Dad," he offered in a weak voice.

"Good, just follow my instructions. Alex, you've got to stand up and then squat down again. Right away! Try to bring your knees to your chest!" This maneuver was designed to redirect blood through the lungs so it could pick up oxygen before returning to the body.

Alex stumbled to his feet with assistance and followed his father's commands without hesitation. Within two minutes the color returned to his face and his sensorium cleared. Sandy let out an audible sigh.

"Close one, huh, Dad?"

"You bet, son. You bet," he replied, clutching Alex in a firm embrace.

"I guess I really need that operation, don't I?"

"Like a camel needs water." This reference made Alex think of his stained shorts. He realized that he had become incontinent during the melee and hoped Sandy hadn't noticed. She had, of course, but made every effort to maintain eye contact with Alex instead of staring at his soaked shorts.

"Dad, I think I've wet my pants," he whispered trembling from the insult of the near-syncopal episode and also from the embarrassment of his clothes wetting.

"Let's get some new stuff at the sports store, you don't want to be sitting in those all day."

Sandy, realizing this was a potentially embarrassing situation, expressed her relief over Alex's recovery and excused herself from the park. On her walk back to town, she realized she harbored true feelings for Alex that went beyond friendship.

Alex bowed his head in embarrassment as the pair returned to town. His father, hoping to lighten the mood, offered some levity.

"That was some excellent squatting back there, son. If you don't make it as a doctor, I think you should apply to gargoyle school, I think you would excel in the field. Ya know, find a nice 'gar-girl' and settle down."

"Funny, Dad! Let's just get this operation over with and get on with our lives." Alex's self-pity was somewhat tempered by the realization that Sandy, at least to some extent, had genuine concern for him during the afternoon's fiasco. He felt, for the first time, that his affections for her were being reciprocated.

Alex selected a new gym outfit from the Ace Sporting Goods store and although his father offered to take him home given the day's events, he declined stating that this was his last real Sunday before the surgery. The pair decided to remain in town for the afternoon and headed toward Aristotle's Greek Café.

Once again, there was no Mr. Aristotle, and the only thing Greek about the restaurant was Nicky Popondopolous, the resident dishwasher. Nevertheless, the walls had arched, wooden panels, which framed frescoes of fishermen reeling in nets as viewed from atop a Mediterranean cliff. Seating consisted of comfortable mahogany booths aligned on one side of the restaurant. The seatbacks reached halfway to the ceiling and were topped with narrow aquariums. It seemed as if particularly slim fish were chosen for these dividers and all colors of the rainbow were represented giving the establishment a very festive feel. Strewn from the ceilings were red wine bottles in wicker baskets alternating with potted fern plants. Located in the back were restrooms with an octopus on the men's door and a stingray on the women's; why these two particular fish were chosen and how an outsider was to decipher which represented which was beyond the scope of Alex's imagination.

The owner, Mr. Collins, led Alex and his father to their seats. He was an extremely pleasant and robust Irishman whose ties to Greece were limited to the gyro stand he worked in as a teenager. His nose was a cherry red stemming from years of drinking. Spider veins coursed across his face resembling a map of the Los Angeles freeway system. A tall white chef's cap sat atop his head although Mr. Collins' s participation in the kitchen was limited to documenting patrons' orders on small slips of paper and submitting them to the actual chef. This guise, however, did lend itself to a quaint café feel and nobody dared challenge his ability to cook. Dr. Harkins started with a Greek salad followed by oysters on the half shell. Alex ordered a Swiss burger cooked very well; he was, by all accounts, the only individual in Mills Creek who was not a seafood eater, which was considered an atrocity in this coastal community.

As the duo was waiting for lunch, the adjoining table was served. This meal included fresh Maine lobster, a dish Alex just didn't understand! How could anyone staring at the lobster as it rested in a bed of lettuce, consume it? As a prepared dish, this delicacy appeared exactly as it did when alive! It looked like an intact organism! How could anyone tear it apart, claw to claw, and shove the fixing down their throat? He supposed if his burger came in the form of a little cow (hooves, eyes, tail, and all) placed within a bun, it would be inedible from a purely aesthetic standpoint. Why was seafood different?

He and his father were eventually served. As they began eating, his father strained to initiate a conversation.

"You know, son," he began tentatively, "there's something I've been meaning to tell you." Alex had an idea where this conversation was going and hastily interrupted, "Dad, you don't have to . . . "

"Let me finish, young man. I know this is a big week for all of us and I've been thinking of you a lot lately. My job mandates that I spend long hours in the hospital and certainly, during my residency, I was never around." His voice was becoming distant. "Anyway, son, I just wanted you to know that although I may not have been physically there for you in the past, my thoughts were always with you and I love you with all my heart, Alex."

The pair became uncomfortable as their eyes met and both shifted their focus to remote objects within the restaurant. Nothing further needed to be vocalized; the message had been conveyed.

Given the afternoon's excitement and Alex's spell, Dr. Harkins decided they would be better off picked up from town in lieu of riding home. Jane Harkins met them at the restaurant thirty minutes later with a bike rack affixed to the family's sport-utility vehicle. Alex loaded the bikes while the bill was paid, and the entire clan headed home.

The house was quiet as Annie and Molly were visiting friends and Evan was put down for a nap after the trip from town. Alex and his parents had a brief rest before focusing their attention and efforts on preparing for the Harkins' Sunday evening tradition: a family barbecue with invitations extended to different individuals on a weekly basis. He and his father were responsible for providing the "grub" and both took the responsibility very seriously.

The barbecue was located on the second floor over the screened porch. This location offered an unhampered view of the neighboring bay and Atlantic Ocean. A double French door connected the deck to the master suite, and was the sole outlet to this area of the house.

The wooden platform had an aged appearance given years of exposure to the elements and, although generally sturdy, contained corners that were somewhat suspect in their ability to support more than twenty pounds. Anyone "in the know" would avoid these regions and hovered in its midportion.

The open hearth itself was set in a casing of stone recovered from the Connecticut shore. Large blocks were piled unceremoniously giving the barbecue an asymmetrical appearance. Paired metal racks suspended transversely across the cooking surface were responsible for supporting the evening's fare. To an outsider, this cooking facility may have appeared rudimentary, but Alex felt that this element of primitiveness gave the outing its inherent charm. Steaks were placed on the upper rack to allow for thorough cooking and the lower tier was reserved for ears of corn and other last-minute dishes.

Igniting the charcoal at the pit's base was always a challenge as ocean gusts regularly quelled freshly lit matches. Alex's grandparents were the first arrivals as the evening's guests filed in without fanfare.

"Hi, Grandpa; how's it going?" He asked excitedly.

"Just fine, lad, and how's me boy?" Alex's heritage on his father's side was purely Anglophile. His grandfather had spent his childhood in Liverpool before relocating to London. To date, his British accent and expressions were unmistakable and remained fodder for Alex's ridicule.

"Ah! Jolly good, old chap, chip-cheerio and all that," Alex quipped, hoping to get a rise from his favorite octogenarian.

"Quit teasing me you pasty-faced little bugger, and give me a hug before I give you a good whipping!"

Alex considered his grandfather an enigma. "British proper" was an understatement and standard attire consisted of a sweater vest, bowtie, and dress shoes. He would never be found in anything less; in fact, dressing casually inferred that the bowtie lacked a pattern. Alex was quite convinced that his grandfather was born wearing a cummerbund and patent leather shoes.

"Really, Grandpa," he continued, "how are things?"

"Well, young man, my health is tip-top and I'm as regular as I've ever been; two bowel movements a day!"

Alex pondered why the elderly fixate so on their bowel habits. He didn't understand this regression to infancy, although he could draw several parallels between the very young and the aged. First, both were candidates for diapers. Second, the acquisition and loss of teeth were of paramount importance, and third, individuals at both ends of the spectrum tended to be wrinkled.

Alex's grandfather approached him as he hovered over the steaks, flipping them intermittently. It was obvious that everyone at the get-together was avoiding the topic of the upcoming operation but his grandfather wished to pursue the subject. "Well, what do you think?"

"About what, Grandpa?"

"Oh, I don't know, lad-about the current economy, the state of the Middle East, famine in Africa, or perhaps, your heart operation!"

"Oh, that."

Alex stared at his grandfather's weather-beaten face. Fine silver hair covered his scalp and touched upon deep wrinkles traversing his forehead. These furrows were derived from years of pensive thought and deliberation and functionally divided the region above the eyebrows into three separate zones. The eyebrows themselves were thick and lacked color as they partially covered his worn blue eyes; a distant and knowing look characterized his eyes and their eighty years of experience.

Large crevices lined the margins of his mouth and accentuated his jowls as they hung symmetrically on either side of his chin. On occasion, during animated moments, his grandfather would speak with such reverence and emotion that drops of saliva would become suspended from his chin giving him the appearance of a rabid bulldog.

Alex had developed an excellent rapport with his grandfather over the years, especially since his father had been so busy, and came to think of him as a friend and confidante.

"I'm really afraid, Grandpa," he replied after great deliberation.

"What's your understanding of your heart condition, lad?"

"Well," Alex began deliberately, "I have a hole in my heart between the two big chambers and a blockage between my heart and lungs. It really didn't get bad until recently. The doctors told me that, with time, the pressure near my lungs has become too high and my heart can't pump blood through them anymore. They said the blood kind of backs up and goes through the hole before receiving oxygen. In fact, that's why I turn blue sometimes, from a lack of oxygen. I know if it doesn't get fixed soon, I will die." He was relieved to be discussing his heart condition on that night. The fact that everyone else was ignoring the topic scared him even more. He paused and reconnected with his grandfather's stare.

"I'm really scared! I'm afraid of the breathing tube they will put down my throat during the operation. What if I wake up and choke on it, how will I breathe? I'm petrified of the needles they'll stick me with and especially terrified of the anesthesia. I've seen on television where people are put to sleep for an operation and they never wake up! I don't want to be in a coma for the rest of my life, Grandpa!" Alex's voice was trembling with fear. He was getting visibly upset and his grandfather thought it a good time to interrupt.

"Listen, lad, plenty of people have these operations every day! You only hear about the horror stories and never the successes. I've had several mates who've had heart surgery and they're all doing fine. As for the anesthesia, it's been perfected over the years and is extremely safe. Your Uncle Seth had a bypass and he's just great. All right, he's a bit of a twit, but I assure you son, he sort of started out that way!" His grandfather hoped a little levity would help Alex's spirits, but his success was limited.

Alex did feel infinitely better, however, after talking with his grandfather. He felt reassured that everything would be fine with the support he had from his family.

The conversation ended but both individuals remained preoccupied throughout the remainder of the evening. Annie and Molly returned home just in time to consume the last two steaks. The twilight was beautiful and the view from the balcony was unparalleled; the ocean seemed to go on forever. Alex glanced across the Atlantic; he realized he was just a small part in the ocean of people's lives and that his story was a minor part of a bigger picture.

The group roasted marshmallows while watching the sunset. Alex beat his father at chess three times before retiring. Tomorrow was reserved for school good-byes. He scanned the room for a final time before shutting the lights off; everything was just as he'd left it that morning and this sense of continuity proved reassuring. The angels over his bed hovered with quiet solace in the darkened room and he drifted off to sleep.

CHAPTER 2

The drive to St. Theresa of Avila School was short as it was located directly behind the parish and adjacent to the schoolyard. It was one of three parochial schools in the area and was considered the most exclusive.

The building itself was a two-story structure composed of deep-red brick and a black wrought-iron fence encircled the grounds separating it from the yard, rectory, and convent. The entrance was an intimidating double wooden door with black iron inlay; at fourteen feet high, these doors made anyone feel small as they passed through. Alex postulated that this was a deliberate equalizer, as if being small was a prerequisite to entering any elementary school.

His mom parked the car in a paved parking lot enclosed in a silver mesh fence. This area was reserved for parking during the morning hours and served as a makeshift play-ground during the afternoons. Alex had fond memories of playing hopscotch as a first and second grader, and eventually dodgeball and 4-square in the latter two years of his schooling.

He reminisced about his dodgeball experience while walking toward the entrance. What a concept! Two teams, separated by an imaginary line, hurling balls at full velocity toward each other. The point, by definition, was to hit the opposing team member with a rubber ball with careless disregard. In fact, bonus points were awarded if the ball struck the head or another vital organ.

He wondered what would happen if adults engaged in this sport. Employees from any corporation could be split in two teams and allowed to injure their opponents (all in good fun, of course). Balls would be hurled back and forth as disgruntled employees targeted their bosses while venting frustration for the day's reprimand. At the sound of the bell, all balls would be placed on the pavement as the employees returned to their workstations. There would be no internalized anger, no regressions, and productivity would increase exponentially. Alex thought the United States Postal Service would benefit most by this outlet in the hopes of quenching potential outbursts from unhappy ex-workers.

The convent and the rectory flanked the school and housed all of Alex's teachers; the majority of the teachers at St. Theresa's were Catholic nuns, although the current principal was a priest. There were two classes in each grade and although it was not common knowledge, students were divided based on academic ability and previous performance. Alex was in 4A, the advanced fourth grade class headed by Sister Agatha.

He and his mom went through the school's main entrance. At the end of the hall was a spiral black staircase in wrought iron which connected the two floors. Kindergarten through third grade were located on the ground floor and fourth through sixth on the upper level. School was in session and each classroom contained between twenty-five to thirty students with a mentor and two student teachers.

Outside the rooms were wooden enclaves containing two-tiered coat racks assigned to the students. Alex's memories of this floor were punctuated by the "disaster drills" during which each student was instructed to assume some posture derivative of the fetal position when an alarm sounding like a sick cow was triggered. Minutes seemed like hours as children ducked their heads between their legs in anticipation of some nuclear holocaust stemming from the cold war which, to the best of his recollection, had ended years ago.

Nevertheless, the exercises continued and the students were taught to fear some unknown foreign threat with new-found nuclear capability and the country du jour was Pakistan. Surely those crazy far-easterners would target Mills Creek with their first guided missile, at least this was the perception of the Catholic gentry in charge.

Fortunately, children located within these oak-lined cubbies were inherently immune from any designated warhead. This protection was further enhanced by layers of outerwear covering their heads as their faces and buttocks became inseparable for an intolerable duration. Invariably, one of the children would assume a position resembling a hibernating yoga instructor at the end of the exercise and would have to be unwound like a soft pretzel being consumed by a ravaged teenager.

Within the infrastructure of the spiral staircase was a two-person elevator which was added to the school recently as a government mandate. Alex usually climbed the staircase on his way to homeroom but wondered how a disability may limit him in the future.

At the base of the steps was the school's cafeteria which amounted to three rows of old-time chairs with attached tabletops, a small refrigeration unit for milk and ice cream, and a blackboard for school announcements. Students were expected to bring their own lunches and dairy products were handed out like a soup kitchen during the depression.

Alex's most vivid memory of that room involved a free-for-all food fight during second grade. This melee was planned and word spread like wildfire from child to child. He prepared accordingly and felt that bologna would make the best projectile. On the eve of the uprising his mom unknowingly packed a bologna and cheese sandwich with cheesecake for heavy artillery. He remembered the event with particular disdain as his uncontrollable laughter resulted in his first desaturation spell. This was truly a bittersweet memory.

At the top of the spiral steps was Alex's old third-grade class. He peered in and saw the children seated attentively with their collective gaze directed toward Sister Mary Catherine, his former teacher. She was truly a wonderful individual who showed deep concern for Alex's condition during their year together.

She was less than five feet tall and weighed close to three hundred pounds making her the same shape from all angles. Having taught for nearly thirty years, Sister Catherine was from the "old school" and wore her habit with great pride and veneration.

Bilateral knee replacements had left her with an asymmetric and strained gait and when viewed from a distance, wearing black dress and habit, she resembled a member of the penguin family. This illusion was reinforced in profile given her sharp chin and beaklike nose and this gained her the dubious distinction of being referred to as "Sister Waddles."

She saw Alex out of the corner of her eye and interrupted her dissertation. "Excuse me children," she said calmly, " I have to visit with a friend." This made him feel wonderful.

"Hello, Alex, I was hoping to see you. You've been in my prayers lately. I'll be thinking of you on Thursday and I know everything will be all right."

"Thank you, sister. It's good to have somebody with "connections" on my side." They both chuckled and this was followed by a very maternal hug. Her eyes welled up as she waddled back to the front of the room.

Alex's fourth-grade class was at the other end of the hall and between the two rooms were more coat racks and lockers. He struggled to remember his combination following the emotional exchange with Sister Catherine but eventually opened his locker. The inside of the door was decorated with cutouts from automobile magazines and pictures of his family.

Within the locker were two inconspicuous brown paper bags and a silver thermos canister; the bags contained Alex's afternoon medication bottles and within the thermos was grape juice.

In the ten minutes between third and fourth period, he was required to take his pills and he had grown quite self-conscious of this activity. As other children were grabbing books for the next class, he would duck his head into the storage area and swallow all four medications at once. This rather large bolus of pills was washed down with a healthy serving of grape juice. The students in the adjacent lockers were generally tolerant of this daily ritual and grew to ignore his unusual behavior.

An asthmatic student from class 4B kept his inhalers in a locker across the hall and had developed his own eccentric techniques in attempts to go unnoticed. Not infrequently, both of them would pop their heads in and out of their lockers at the same time resembling paired chickens grasping for feed. When their eyes met after "feeding time", a casual wink usually followed.

After gathering his belongings Alex headed for the fourth-grade class. To his surprise a large banner was draped across the front blackboard and read, "Good luck, Alex." Each student had inscribed his name and a brief message along the banner and this outpouring of generosity made him quite emotional. He pushed back the tears and entered the room.

"Well hello, Alex, we've been expecting you," Sister Agatha exclaimed practically jumping from her chair as she saw him enter. "How do you like the banner? The children loved making it for you. We've also made some cupcakes and punch; come and have some."

The children abandoned their daily lessons briefly and joined Alex in a treat. Although he was grateful for the gesture, the whole thing seemed like a final sendoff. Weren't they planning to see him again?

Sister Agatha motioned Alex to approach her. She was the Stan Laurel to Sister Catherine's Hardy. Barely over ninety pounds, her hands were devoid of fat and one could almost count the thirteen bones of her wrist. In fact, when the two nuns walked together in the halls, they resembled the number 10.

As he met her, she placed an object in his palm and he closed his hands around it. The offering was not discernible by simple palpation but as he pulled away he released his grasp. She handed him a pair of antique rosary beads and a baseball card autographed by Reggie Jackson. An explanation was obviously necessary.

"The rosary beads," she began, "were given to me on the first day I entered the order. Can you imagine, Alex, how many times I've rolled them in my hands as I prayed for someone's well being? And you know what, they've never failed me. It's your turn; you take them with you to Hitchcock and use them before the operation. The card was given to me by Reggie Jackson himself. I don't know if it's lucky, but it couldn't hurt, right?" What an absurd combination of gifts, he thought, but it was like holding the magic of a genie's lamp in his hand.

"You give those back to me after the operation, you hear?" she insisted.

"I will, sister. If I can't for some reason my parents will . . ." Alex stuttered.

"Stop that right now," Sister Agatha's voice became stern, "you will bring those back to me yourself!" This condemnation was her way of showing him affection and was more efficacious than Sister Catherine's hug.

"You bet."

The drive home was uneventful. The entire family enjoyed a quiet dinner as plans were discussed for the following day's travel. Alex and his mother would be the first to leave and his father would join them the night prior to surgery. Both grandparents would be moving to the house temporarily to oversee the girls and Evan.

He began packing after dinner with the assistance of his mother. "You'll need several sets of pajamas, slippers, toiletries, and plenty of reading material," his mother advised. His father reminded him not to forget the chess set or the gift he received from Mr. McKinley. Normally, packing for a trip was exciting but on this occasion he dreaded every minute. Do people on death row have to pack a toothbrush, he wondered?

This chore was finally completed and his parents left to pack their own bags. Alex declined a final opportunity to play chess and opted for a more introspective evening. He lay still, staring at the ceiling, and prayed like never before. Sister Agatha's rosary beads had found their way into his bed and, inexplicably, Reggie Jackson's likeness was propped against his pillow keeping him company. Who would have thought that a cardboard picture of a baseball player striking a batting stance would provide comfort to a scared child? The good sister obviously knew what she was doing.

The next morning began with the piercing wail of Alex's mom as she yelled for him to "come downstairs right away, or else". His procrastination was protracted as the feather pillow and patchwork quilt seemed exceptionally comfortable.

Unfortunately, Reggie had suffered a near-fatal crush injury overnight as Alex failed to remove him prior to sleeping. The resulting insult left poor Mr. Jackson folded in half and dripping with the saliva of an eleven year old in dreamland. There was no doubt, given his ability to face adversity in the past, that Mr. October would make a complete recovery and eventually come to enjoy his first foray out of the convent.

He lumbered down the circular staircase as if he were reenacting the Crucifixion before entering the kitchen. Awaiting him were four family members with ear-to-ear grins and the reflection from their teeth could have supplied enough solar energy for a small community in Missouri.

"What's going on?" he asked suspiciously. "What's with the stool-eating grins?"

On the table was Alex's favorite breakfast-Chinese egg rolls, cold pizza, twizzlers, and chocolate Èclairs.

"Why are you all sitting on the same side of the table facing me? What is this, the Last Supper or something? Is this my last meal? If it is, how about a blindfold and a cigarette, I've always wanted to try one."

"Relax, son," his dad chimed in, "the girls wanted to give you a send-off and cracking a bottle of champagne on your head just didn't seem fitting. Similarly, scrambled eggs and bacon seemed inappropriate so pipe down and enjoy the treat. And if you did have a cigarette, you'd probably turn as blue as your grandmother's hair, so why don't you aspire for something higher?"

The family catered to Alex this morning and although he didn't want to be the target of their pity, it was great to feel all the love that surrounded him. The bags were loaded unceremoniously into the back of the truck as he and his mom headed for the airport. The good-byes were kept to a minimum and his sisters maintained their sense of decorum as they pushed back tears. As the car pulled away, Alex glanced into the passenger rearview mirror. Annie and Molly had lost their composure and were last seen being cradled by their father with faces buried in his arms. The crying was almost audible and he was proud of them for staying strong in his presence. He began sniffling himself and this did not go unnoticed by his mother.

"I know you'll miss the girls, dear" she said softly, "but you'll be home before you know it. This whole miserable experience will be a memory soon."

The road to the airport completely bypassed the town and en route Alex caught a glimpse of St. Theresa's steeple. He wished he were sitting in his miserable little classroom behind his antiquated desk-chair listening to Sister Agatha's incessant drone. Anything would be better than feeling the pain from a big cut and the division of his breastbone. What if he didn't heal properly?, he thought, as this new complication popped into his head for the first time. What if his breastbone fell apart and his heart had no covering? This vision sent a visible chill through his bones and alerted his mother to distract him.

"There it is, Mills Creek International Airport," she said excitedly.

International airport, what a joke, Alex thought to himself. The only thing international about this airport was the Taco Bell in the airport's food court and the one flight a day destined for Montreal, Canada. He thought it quite interesting that any municipal airstrip with a semblance of a runway longer than two hundred yards could qualify for this auspicious designation.

Most flights departing from the Mills Creek heliport-on-steroids, as he called it, were in twin-prop planes which he termed flying coffins. Fortunately, their flight today was on a real jet airplane, albeit small, with real-life stewardesses and a pilot wearing a uniform. This came as a huge relief to him as they boarded the flight.

Northeast Airlines flight 248 was relatively full on this occasion and most of its occupants were businessmen and professionals. Alex and his mother felt somewhat out of place dressed in casual attire while the rest of the passengers were in working clothes. The man next to him was reading *The New England Journal of Medicine* and was most likely a physician. Practically everyone else in their row was working on a laptop computer and, as he glanced laterally, he had the feeling he was at a major sporting event among the sports reporters.

The captain's voice came overhead as the passenger doors were closed. He informed them that the short flight would take approximately one hour and ten minutes as the skies were calm. Following this, a stewardess presented a brief safety video and warned that electronic devices were no longer allowed until after takeoff. There was an audible moan from the laptop users and most looked liked children being called for dinner as they put away their computers. Alex could almost hear it, "C'mon Mom, just five more minutes . . . please."

The takeoff was unremarkable and the computer nerds had reinitiated their typing before the landing gear was retracted. Several minutes later an announcement came overhead, "There will now be a snack provided along with our complimentary beverage service so please remain in your seats as the trays come around."

This news was received by the passengers as if it were more important than the moon landing. Alex scanned the plane and was amused at the sight of all these proper professionals as they sat up in anticipation of "the snack". It seemed as if they had never been fed before.

Complete silence was observed as the trays came around. One by one plastic bags containing between twelve and fifteen lightly salted peanuts were distributed to the obedient lot and he could swear the doctor next to him was panting like a dog awaiting a reward for a successful trick.

The imagery was further enhanced by the lady sitting one

seat across and diagonal to him. She looked like a seal in profile and this visual was solidified by three fine hairs emanating from a mole on the corner of her mouth. As the food cart approached, Alex's imagination got the best of him and he was almost sure she barked for food and then clapped after consuming the seal chow. He couldn't help but laugh out loud.

Finally it was his turn. He sarcastically cradled the bag of peanuts in both hands as if handling a newborn as he transferred the package from the stewardess's basket onto his tray table.

"Would you like a drink, young man?" she asked respectfully.

"Yes, please ma'am, I'd like a soda."

She began pouring the beverage and continued, "Would you like the whole can?"

Alex stared back blankly. He whispered to his mother, "We've just paid three hundred dollars each for this one-hour plane ride and she wants to give half my can to the guy behind me. You've got to be kiddin' me."

"Yes please ma'am, I believe I could enjoy the entire can if given the chance," he said smugly.

"Alex, stop it. Have you lost your mind? Where'd you leave your manners, on the beach?" his mother scolded.

"I'm sorry Mom, but this stuff is crackin' me up. These airline people must think we're idiots." The remainder of the flight went smoothly but the final insult came just before landing.

"Ladies and gentlemen," the stewardess interrupted overhead, " the captain has informed me that we are on our final approach to Hitchcock International Airport. Please raise your seat backs and tray tables and put away any electronic devices currently in use." Another audible moan.

The flight crew came around and reprimanded those individuals who had slept through the announcement and defied the authorities by maintaining a reclining position. Alex was guilty as charged and he thought this the most ridiculous air regulation of them all. Apparently, if a collision were imminent, passengers were to assume the crash position which, implicitly, meant perfectly upright. The premise was, he assumed, that the fine line between life and death in an airplane crash was drawn somewhere between the uncomfortable upright seated position and a very comfortable partially reclined position. In other words, the defining stance between survival and death was the six inches of possible repose offered by the seat backs.

If it were up to him, he pondered, passengers would be encouraged to be as comfortable as possible as the end approached. He could hear the loudspeaker announcement now, "Ladies and gentlemen, Captain Alex has informed me that the plane is in peril and a crash is inevitable. With that in mind, we encourage you to recline as far back as possible and suggest you put your feet up on the seats in front of you. Feel free to remove your shoes and loosen your belts. Since this will most likely be a fatal crash, we will be distributing the remainder of our peanut snacks and beverages so that you may go out with a bang. In case of a water landing, your seat backs will serve as flotation devices and in this instance, just prior to impact, we suggest you carefully position yourselves with your chest against your thighs and head between your knees in a crouching position. Those of you so inclined may take the liberty of kissing your butts good-bye . . . "

Once again Alex laughed out loud; he was really amusing himself on this plane ride.

"Are you losing your mind?" his mother joked. The craziness of the flight had distracted Alex nicely from the thought of his upcoming surgery.

The landing was perfect and the plane disembarked at gate 7. Hitchcock Airport was basically two glorified plane hangars connected by a sidewalk. The baggage carousel was located in the furthest building and was attended by a burly man in orange overalls. He assisted with their luggage and instructed them that the medical center was easily a twenty-minute ride by car. The pair exited the facility and hailed a taxi.

The driver's side door read Hitchcock Cab Company. The automobile was supposed to be a neon yellow, in traditional cab fashion, resembling those found in every major city.

Unfortunately, it had large areas of rust over each wheel well and the decrepitation was so extensive that the car appeared to be brown in color with islands of yellow between rust pockets.

The cabbie carelessly drove onto the sidewalk with his front wheels as he rushed to pick up his fare. Thoughtfully, he exited the car and opened the trunk before assisting with loading the luggage. All three individuals then entered the vehicle with the passengers seated in back. Alex examined the interior of the cab. It was clearly as old on the inside as its outward appearance and the seats had alternating bands of faded vinyl and foam packing. The rear ashtray was full to the brim with discarded ashes and he supposed the fallout from the Mount St. Helen's eruption must have been neater.

The plastic divider separating the seats was riddled with warning stickers and No Smoking signs. Obviously, the literacy campaign did not make a stop in Hitchcock.

Affixed to the passenger's side visor was the driver's taxi license. Alex had to squint to make out the name. It read Ivan Czynkowisk.

"Hey Mom," he asked, "do you think there is a stipulation in the United Brotherhood of Cab Guys manual that states that you have to have more consonants than vowels in your name, and that it has to start with five of them in a row before you can qualify for driving? I mean, where do they find these guys? Perhaps they should all head over to Hawaii where they have an overabundance of vowels and strike a deal."

His mother ignored him although she was fighting back laughter. She would let him continue the sarcasm for now realizing it was probably an outlet for his stress, no matter how obnoxious it was.

"And look at the way the guy's dressed," Alex just wouldn't stop. " I mean, faded cockney cap, a half-eaten cigar in his mouth, six layers of flannel clothes, and shoes that Charlie Chaplin wouldn't wear. I mean, is there a dress code for these guys? I bet if you stopped any random cabbie in New York City, he'd be wearing exactly the same thing. And look at that stubble on his face! Maybe we should introduce him to "Mr. Razor" and . . . "

"All right, that's enough, young man. I've had it with your incessant sarcasm. If you're nervous or scared that's one thing, but it's going to stop right now!" His mother had had it. She looked out the window once again and wondered if there really was a cab guys brotherhood.

Ridgewood Children's Hospital was located on the outskirts of Hitchcock and the road leading there from the airport went directly through town. Hitchcock was quite similar to Mills Creek in size but because its primary industry was nearby Hitchcock College, downtown consisted of alternating pubs and fast-food restaurants.

At any hour, the main thoroughfare was congested with

some fraction of the thirty thousand underclassmen who overtook the town every fall. Being June, the school was in its last trimester and as the outside temperatures rose, class attendance dropped precipitously. On this particular day Alex and his mother were amazed at the casual friendliness of the area and marveled at the atrocities in clothing this year's student body fashioned as the cab drove by.

As the thoroughfare left downtown, he caught a glimpse of a tall glass tower which he identified correctly as belonging to the children's hospital. The road connecting the municipality to this massive facility was windy and tree lined. It felt like entering the Black Forest in Germany as the taxi coursed through the woodlands.

After approximately seven miles of beautiful scenery, a sign was posted marking the entrance to the Ridgewood campus. It wasn't readily obvious why such a prestigious institution should be located in the boonies, but after reading the hospital's brochure it became obvious that a very large endowment from the Aston family facilitated its construction. This New Hampshire-based dynasty made a fortune in the railroad industry during the nineteenth century and this "old" money was destined to remain within the state. When Elizabeth Aston gave birth to a baby with malrotation of the foregut (a congenital malformation of the intestines that was almost invariably fatal until recently), she committed herself and a large portion of her inheritance to providing care for small children and, therein, established the Ridgewood Children's Hospital.

Over the years the reputation of this fine institution grew exponentially. Its scenic setting, access to the wilderness, and lack of a big city feel proved appealing to numerous physicians who were renowned leaders in their fields. With time, it compiled an unparalleled staff of experts who set the standards for care in the medical profession. On a more personal level, Alex's father had done a fellowship with the pediatric cardiac surgeon who would be performing his surgery and the entire family had complete confidence in the Hitchcock health system.

As he saw the sign at the entrance, Alex's heart dropped. The time was here. No more planning; no more waiting; no more spells. This day always seemed like a mark on a calendar, a milestone for the future, and a topic for conversation, but now it was here. This event, like many other life-defining moments, carried with it so much hopeful anticipation that actuality proved to be a near cathartic experience. Jane Harkins found herself clenching the armrest of the taxi with such vigor that her hands turned white. Her little boy was going to be repaired.

CHAPTER 3

The Hitchcock campus was sprawling. They both thought it best to be dropped off at the Hitchcock Inn before taking a shuttle to the main hospital. The cabbie pulled onto the circular drive in front of the hotel and, true to form, rolled onto the sidewalk with his front wheels. The only thing they don't teach at cabbie school is driving, Alex thought, and was proud for not saying it out loud.

The pair checked into adjoining rooms and unpacked without fanfare. The remainder of the day would be filled by registration formalities including preoperative blood work, and Alex dreaded this the most. He had no problem looking at other people's blood or substitutes used in gory television shows, but the sight of his own blood made him feel weak in the knees, even more so than Sandy Cromwell.

The knock on the door was his mother and she instructed him to meet her in the lobby in ten minutes. To distract himself, Alex flipped through the preprogrammed television stations and on channel 11 found an instructional film detailing the hospital registration process. It was ironic how darn happy everyone seemed on the film, even the patients having blood drawn. This must have been staged, he concluded, as it was unfathomable that the ten year old depicted in the video could actually enjoy having a large needle stuck in his vein. It was time to head to the lobby and he pocketed his rosary beads and baseball card before meeting his mother at the front desk.

"When will the next shuttle be leaving for the main hospital, ma'am?" she asked the reception clerk.

"We have no designated shuttles, Miss, but the monorail arrives every eight minutes at the rear of the building and will transport you free of charge."

Monorails! Alex thought to himself. What is this, Disneyland or something? He half expected the security guard at the hospital to be dressed in a red suit with large black ears atop his head and, perhaps, his physicians would be Snow White's dwarfs. "Gee, I hope I get Doc," he whispered under his breath.

The monorail itself was quite magnificent. Straddling a two-foot beam containing electrical power connections, it seemed to hover above the ground and, at times, actually did. The ride was smooth as silk as the bullet-shaped projectile carrying fourteen individuals swept around the Hitchcock campus. Stops were frequent and included the main parking lot, John Wayne Cancer Center, the Hitchcock hospital employee day care center, and finally the train station for the main facility. It was truly an impressive means of transportation and it was obvious the hospital was well funded.

"Maybe we should go around again, Mom," Alex volunteered, as his nerves were getting the better of him. "Ya know, to get the lay of the land and stuff." She grabbed his hand as his anxiety was clearly palpable and ushered him up the terminal steps into the hospital's main lobby.

It was an absolutely amazing site. Floor-to-ceiling windows sparkled as they spanned three floors along the length of the front facade giving the lobby the appearance of a Mormon tabernacle. Brass shelves lined the perimeter of the walls at each floor's demarcation and housed enormous stuffed animals donated by a local toy company. Two stuffed lions measuring ten feet high stood guard at the front entrance as a tribute to Mann's Chinese Theater in Hollywood.

Directly across from the front desk were paired glass elevators. They were cast in iron and afforded a 270-degree view to the passenger. The two lifts were immediately side by side and appeared to be racing if the exact combination of floors were pressed at exactly the right time. It seemed as if the leftmost of the two elevators was partially reserved for frequent fliers, e.g., those children with extensive stays in the hospital who thought of the glass enclosures as a ride rather than an alternative to the stairs. On this particular occasion, it was bursting with small patients and their IV poles. To the casual observer, it could easily have resembled a Disney ride therein complementing the monorail.

A walled-off section adjacent to the registration desk contained several red wagons which had also been donated. These chariots were reserved for the transportation of sick children in hopes of sparing them the monotony of the medical wards, at least for a brief period of time.

The "regulars" would decorate their wagons like a child would his bicycle and even the IV poles attached to their backs supported flags and team pennants. As the parents of these children became acquainted, they would travel throughout the facility in packs resembling motorcycle gangs as they terrorized the hospital wings. Alex thought the inevitable progression would be young patients in leather jackets with emblems such as Heck's Angels or the Ridgewood Riders sarcastically embroidered on their backs.

Along the perimeter of this magnificent entryway was located a trough of water measuring two feet wide and twelve inches deep. Several canals were interconnected in the middle of the foyer in a starlike fashion not unlike the Champs-Elysees in Paris. Small arched wooden bridges were numerous throughout the lobby and allowed visitors to climb over these pint-sized Venetian canals. The miniature gondolas moored at the corners of the troughs were for decoration only.

The pièce de résistance was a large fountain directly in the middle of the atrium which rose ten feet high and was lit in various colors. Over time, this had developed into a sort of a wishing well and routinely visitors could be seen tossing change into the fountain hoping to sway a loved one's hospital course in a favorable direction. These coins were collected on a monthly basis and used to buy toys and reading material for some of the less fortunate children. In this way, hope was recycled continuously.

It was finally Alex's turn at the lobby desk and, after filling out the preliminary paperwork, the receptionist directed them to the preoperative testing area for blood work. This office was located on the second floor and afforded him his first of many opportunities to ride the glass elevators. Once on board he began to appreciate the size of the main lobby and its beauty. It really did have a fantasy quality, like a theme park, and it struck him that this effect was intentional. The surroundings made him feel at ease and he was sure younger visitors would feel the same.

As the elevator rose, a small cafeteria and McDonald's came into view in front of which was a large replica of the company's lovable clown. His mother assured him they would go there for a late lunch after the afternoon's activities. The remainder of the day would be spent in preadmission testing and touring the pediatric intensive care unit (PICU).

Riding in the elevator with him was what appeared to be a two-year-old child in one of the red wagons. This youngster had been through a war, Alex thought, as he scrutinized the child before him. The child's arms were riddled with puncture sites and old bruises and his left forearm was splinted in a brace to ensure that the current IV remained in place. The board supporting this precious little extremity was tattered and the bandages holding the whole contraption together were stained from previous blood draws.

He felt an inexplicable urge to rip the apparatus off the little boy's arms and set him free like a deer in captivity. The young patient offered only the saddest of glances as he raised his eyes to meet Alex's. They contained a vacant stare, one that stems from an inability to understand a situation and the futility of not being able to change it. What had this poor child done in his short life to deserve any of this?, Alex wondered. This visual helped him realize that there were others who were much worse off than he and his self-pity seemed almost inappropriate.

The elevator doors opened and the little child was wheeled out first. Alex and his mother followed and headed toward the preoperative testing office. Upon entering, they were greeted by a young lady dressed in a traditional nurse's outfit with a carousel pin on her lapel. This was the official Ridgewood emblem and identified all hospital employees. The carousel symbolized the circle of life in a context a child could appreciate.

"May I help you, folks?"

"Yes, this is my son, Alex, and he is scheduled to have

open-heart surgery later this week," his mom replied. The office was cold and sterile and unlike the rest of the hospital, it contained very few adornments. Within the confines of the room was a waiting area, reception desk, several chairs with built-in armrests for blood drawing, and a bathroom. There was no doubt this part of the hospital was all business.

"Ah, yes, Mr. Harkins. I have you penned in for this Thursday. You will be Dr. Addison's second case and are scheduled to start at eleven in the morning. We will need a full complement of blood work, a chest x-ray, and an EKG. Fortunately, there's no wait and as soon as I can print out some labels, we'll begin the blood draw."

The term "complement" struck Alex as funny as there was nothing flattering about the blood-drawing process. The term "draw" seemed similarly unsuitable as he was clearly the loser in this transaction.

"All right young man, I'm ready for you."

"That makes one of us," he mouthed as he dragged his feet across the room into the bloodletting chair. "Didn't they abandon this practice in the Medieval period," he asked jokingly, "and there aren't going to be any leeches, are there?"

The nurse, like her surroundings, was all business. There was no hint of a sense of humor and her seriousness belied her youthful age. This proved quite unnerving and Alex began to fidget in his chair. He named her Brun Helga, for lack of a better moniker since her identification tag was unintelligible. She reached into a drawer and pulled out several collection tubes of different colors and a venipuncture set.

Alex began to tremble visibly and Helga made no efforts to put him at ease. She continued methodically with impressive efficiency and given her no-frills attitude and paucity of wasted movements, Helga was the prodigal blood-drawing machine and could have given Arnold Schwarzenegger's Terminator a run for his money.

"This is going to pinch a little bit."

The pinch was more like a full stab as the large-bore needle was thrust into his disproportionately small vein.

"Yikes," he screamed as if he were in a bad out-take from a "Scooby Doo" rerun. "Man, that smarts."

"Almost done," Helga said without moving her mouth, "two more vials."

The blood kept flowing as Alex intermittently looked at the contraption in his arm wondering if he would shrivel up like a dry prune when the bloodletting was over.

"Well, at least it's not blue." he said making a casual reference to his heart condition.

"If it were, young man," the robot replied, " you would be

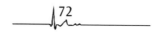

going to the operating room today instead of Thursday."

With this remark one of the corners of Helga's mouth turned upward as if she were trying to smile but was limited by the plaster of Paris her young and emotionless face was set in. This little taste of human expression completely relaxed Alex and although he was still feeling lightheaded, he felt the world was going to be okay.

As he got up from the chair, he became faint and fell backward into the seat. Sweat poured from his face and his hands were clammy. Helga rushed into action and took his blood pressure and pulse which were 110/60 and 43, respectively.

"A little bradycardic," she said, "a sit-down will take care of that." She handed him a box of orange juice realizing the beverage and rest period would make him feel better.

Alex and his mom were directed to another office for an electrocardiogram. Twelve small pads were strewn across his chest, affixed by a weak adhesive, and connected to the EKG machine across the room. A paper scrolled out one end of the apparatus like a ticker tape at the stock market. The technician casually glanced at the tracing and, although not a physician, he had seen so many of them that he was able to pick out aberrations routinely. He studied the technician's face with his fists clenched hoping not to see a reaction. He was pleased when the paper was ripped off the machine and placed in his file unceremoniously.

They were then directed to the nursing supervisor's office at the pediatric intensive care unit. A collection of parents and their children had gathered there and were set to have a tour of the floor as a prelude to upcoming surgery. The head nurse approached the group and introduced herself. She was clad in rose-colored scrubs with the Ridgewood carousel embroidered on her left shirt pocket. Her eyes were a stunning blue and her sharp and attractive face was framed by straight, shoulder-length blonde hair with strawberry highlights. She had the figure of a model and this could not be hidden by the shapeless outfit assigned to her. Her nail color matched the outfit as did the clogs she wore on her feet. The confidence she possessed was apparent in her gait as she approached her office.

"Good afternoon, ladies and gentlemen, and welcome to Ridgewood Children's Hospital's intensive care unit. You're all here for a preoperative introduction to our floor and we hope that by the end of the afternoon, all your questions will have been answered. As for the children in the group, you are all about to have surgery with us and I hope some of the mystery and fears surrounding this experience will seem less worrisome after the tour. Now then, my name is nurse Renee McKenzie and I am in charge of the daily goings-on in this unit. The age of our patients varies from one day to sixteen years and all of our kids are fresh postops. The average duration of stay is 2 to 3 days and varies with each procedure performed. I hope not to scare you today and please feel free to ask questions as we go along. Follow me."

Alex was as scared as he'd ever been. This was it; this was

what his family had been talking about for the last two years. He was about to get a glimpse of what he'd look like after the operation. The entire group consisted of four children and six parents; there were only two fathers present and he would've given anything to have his dad by his side.

The doors to the ward opened automatically as Nurse McKenzie led the others in. The rooms were arranged in a horseshoe fashion so that all beds could be seen from the central nurse's station. There were no walls between rooms, rather glass doors; if a particularly sick child needing extracorporeal life support was in the PICU, the glass partitions between adjacent rooms could be opened to allow for an effective doubling in room size. For privacy, plain brown curtains could be drawn on either side of the doors and this was especially important when parents slept with their recovering children.

Directly above the nurse's station was a series of thirteen monitors displaying the vital signs of each room's inhabitants. The technology was impressive and was reminiscent of the command deck of an intergalactic spaceship. The entire setup would have been quite interesting to Alex if he didn't know its real purpose.

Numerous individuals could be seen milling within the unit and their uniforms helped in their identification. The nurses wore scrubs of various colors and some wore scrub jackets adorned with the faces of small cartoon children in an effort to keep things light for the young patients. The respiratory therapists could be identified by their blue scrub outfits, whereas laundry and janitorial personnel were allocated orange denim overalls.

The physicians had their own fashion hierarchy. Medical students could be seen in their short white coats and those who aspired to become surgeons, at least for the time being, would cover themselves in operative attire. The interns, known as first-year residents-in-training, also wore short lab coats but could be unequivocally distinguished by their weary faces and unkempt appearance. Those at a higher level of training and attending doctors sported full-length white coats and rarely wore scrubs outside the operating room. Any combination of the aforementioned individuals could be seen in the PICU at all hours of the day.

The tour group stopped at the first room and the sight took Alex by surprise. On the walls were hand-painted murals of circus life and beach scenes but there was no mistaking this room was intended for the postoperative management of critically ill children. Mounted in the corner was a monitor which, upon first glance, could have easily been erroneously identified as a television but was, in fact, a vitals monitor. There were three rows of multicolored tracings labeled blood pressure, central venous pressure, and oxygen saturations from top to bottom. Each was scrolling across the screen and only the topmost tracing had any significant variation.

The sounds of the room were similarly unmistakable. Each heartbeat was audible as an intermittent beep which faded gradually between tones and the ventilator interrupted regularly with its respiratory excursions not unlike the Darth Vader character in the Star Wars trilogy. Ironically, in the background were the sounds of a baseball game. A father was situated in a lounge chair next to his child watching a ceiling-mounted television above the room's doorway.

The anxious parent stood abruptly as if he were the host at a party in which the guests arrived unexpectedly early. He fumbled to straighten himself before being interrupted by Nurse McKenzie.

"I'm sorry, Mr. Wong," she started. " I hope you don't mind. These families are taking a tour of our unit just like you did before Sun Lee had her operation."

"No fears, Ms. McKenzie," he replied in broken English as he reflexively bowed to the group. " We are thrilled with the care our little one is receiving and would like to help in any way possible." After stating his intentions, he politely sat back in his seat and returned to the game.

Alex's eyes were fixated on the small infant contained within the incubator at the center of the room. The child was under an ultraviolet heat lamp and wrapped in layers of blankets in order to maintain an adequate temperature. Only the face and one arm were visible.

Still on a ventilator, a pencil-sized tube remained perpendicular to the child's face as it connected with the breathing machine at the bedside. Her eyes were intentionally covered in protective glasses which wrapped around her face in an effort to protect her from the UV irradiation from the lamp. Two plastic chest tubes could be seen exiting the midportion of the blanket and were draining a fluid the color of Kool-Aid. A miniature bladder catheter was also visible as it connected to a urometer at the edge of the incubator.

As the child writhed, she eventually became unraveled from the blanket cocoon and a small foot with a large intravenous line poked through. A footboard kept the extremity immobilized at the ankle and the whole contraption appeared quite barbaric to the uneducated observer in this case, Alex.

To his eyes, the baby was fighting the breathing tube as if she were uncomfortable or choking, and this was one of Alex's biggest fears for himself. Nurse McKenzie had seen the look on his face before and decided this would be a good time for some explanations.

"As you can see," she began quite deliberately, "this neonate is two days out from her corrective heart surgery and remains intubated. Although it appears Sun Lee is fighting the endotracheal tube, she is, in fact, trying to feed using a very natural reflex found in children her age. I can guarantee you that she is in no pain and will have no recollection of this event."

It was as if she'd read his mind. Alex couldn't have asked for a more timely explanation and, at least temporarily, his fear was quelled. He quickly glanced over the myriad of IV pumps mounted on poles surrounding the neonate's incubator. This tour was not at all comforting to him and he wished it were over. As Nurse McKenzie continued her dissertation she was abruptly interrupted by an overhead announcement.

"Code blue, pediatric intensive care unit; code blue PICU."

Before the message could be completed, people were rushing in the direction of room seven.

Nurse McKenzie glanced at the desk clerk and asked, " Is that the switch from yesterday?" referring to the newborn who underwent an arterial switch procedure by Dr. Addison's assistant earlier in the week.

"Naw," replied the morbidly obese clerk as she continued to file her nails undisturbed. "I reckon that's Addison's truncus from Friday." Alex was dumbstruck by the lack of emotion this clerk displayed in a time of crisis and the fact that patients were referred to by their procedures rather than their names. Nevertheless, he was caught up in the exhilaration of the moment and found himself migrating, quite unintentionally, in the direction of the room. The rest of the group appeared to be paralyzed in fear and remained in place.

The scene around room seven could best be described as organized chaos. Short lab coats were mixed with blue scrubs and long white coats. People in orange reflexively stepped away from the melee. It appeared that one of the interns was first on the scene and was over the bed of a three-year-old child. He was barking out orders in a trembling voice as individuals entering the room donned protective masks and gowns.

"Another amp of epi, stat," he shouted trying to appear confident, "chase that with an amp of bicarb, a code dose of calcium, and I want the fluids wide open."

All the while, Dr. Einthoven, the attending cardiologist, stood in the corner of the room and shook his head at the head nurse if he wanted the orders obeyed. A large red mechanics cart containing drugs, an intubation setup, and defibrillator had taken up residence outside the room. As the young doctor continued his onslaught of orders, no less than five nurses were passing vials of drugs and solutions to the head nurse whose responsibility it was to do the actual injecting. In the corner of the room was a young nurse carrying a clipboard and documenting the details of the code as they developed. This was the official transcript that would be reviewed analytically after the event.

"Does anyone feel a pulse?" Dr. Einthoven shouted as the tracing on the monitor resembled a series of mountain peaks in succession, " I think the patient is fibrillating. Did anyone get in touch with Addison?"

This particular rhythm was ominous and the group of nurses stood away from the bed instinctively. The crash cart was rolled in from the hall and the intern grabbed the paddles on the defibrillator. "Clear," he shouted, as contact pads were placed on the child's sternum. In a flash, he delivered 360 joules of electricity to the chest and the tiny body jumped out of bed in a quick jerk.

"Nothing," said Einthoven. " Shock him again."

This order was followed by two more attempts at defibrillation without success. More drugs and electrolytes were administered and chest compressions had been initiated. Although the child was barely thirty pounds, the intern placed both knees on the side of the bed and used his body weight for additional leverage. Even with this assistance, he wasn't seeing the appropriate deflections on the blood pressure tracing and looked at Einthoven for guidance.

"Your compressions are not effective," Einthoven stated flatly. "Can someone get in touch with Addison, damn it."

With this utterance Dr. Addison entered the unit. "I'm sorry, Boris," he said, looking in Einthoven's direction, "I was scrubbed in the OR and I was on pump. Came as soon as I could. What have we got here?"

The scenario was explained to him by the attending cardiologist. "Sounds bad, guys," he responded matter-of-factly, "and I agree that your compressions aren't cutting it. We better crack this chest. Someone get me the chest tray."

The sternal set was essentially a makeshift operative tray and one was located behind the nurse's desk. It contained all the instruments necessary to perform a minor heart procedure at the bedside.

Dr. Addison quickly gowned and gloved while a nurse took over the chest compressions. Another assistant placed his magnifying loupes over his eyes and these were connected to a headlight. A scrub technician made her way over from the operating room and began to assist him.

"Someone throw some Betadine on that chest," Dr. Addison ordered as he reached for the scalpel, "and you keep doing compressions till I tell you to stop."

All the while the child's parents had been standing in the corner of the room and had gone unnoticed. The sight of the scalpel in Addison's hands was too much for the mother and she let out a piercing wail that caught everyone's attention.

Dr. Addison paused as the knife was about to touch skin and said, "Someone please escort the family from the room." This was facilitated by one of the nursing assistants and the parents were led to the critical care waiting area.

"All right, stop your compressions."

Within a second, the knife blade went through skin and subcutaneous tissues and the sternal wires were visible. "Wire cutters," he barked as these were placed in his hand. The chest was opened and a small retractor inserted spreading both halves of the breastbone.

"This heart is full," shouted Addison, "stop your fluids. More epi and bicarb." He placed his hand within the chest and cupped the little boy's heart. Internal cardiac massage was instituted as his hand replaced the contractile function of the organ within it. "C'mon, buddy, c'mon."

This continued for what seemed like an eternity and all the while multiple vials of drugs and electrolytes were administered. All at once Addison terminated the massage. He looked up at the monitor and saw a tracing and a blood pressure.

"It's a start. Go up on your epi-cal and titrate in a little levophed, girls."

The pressure continued to rise and at one point became too high. The nurses were instructed to back off on their vasopressors and the room let out a collective sigh of relief.

After a few more minutes, as the patient continued to stabilize, Dr. Addison informed Renee that he would be taking the child back to the operating room for chest closure.

"That was a close one, Mark. What do you think happened?" she asked.

"Probably some air in one of the lines got into a coronary artery, Renee; make sure your girls are diligent about flushing them. Nice response though, you know, with the code and all."

He winked at her as he headed in the direction of the operating suite and she blushed like a schoolgirl. Dr. Addison was a good-looking man and one would have to be blind not to notice the attraction between the pair. They had dated when he was a resident and the relationship fizzled for unknown reasons. The mutual attraction was as strong as ever.

Nurse McKenzie headed back to the action to supervise the transfer of the patient to the operating room. On her way, she glanced down the hallway and was startled to see a frazzled group of individuals huddling together for comfort.

"Oh my god," she whispered to herself, "I totally forgot about the tour."

As she approached the assembly she felt obligated to offer an explanation. "I can assure you," she offered tentatively, "that our young patient is going to be fine. Although you've seen nothing else, our unit is usually quite uneventful and verges on being boring." This comment fell on deaf ears as a sea of empty stares converged on her. "In any case, I hope this has been an adequate introduction to our facility and I will be happy to field any questions at this time."

Again no response. She thought it best to lead the group back to the main lobby and call it a day. As she headed in that direction, the muted crowd followed like sheep after being shorn. Eventually they reached the atrium and the group dispersed. Alex and his mother headed toward the monorail. Inexplicably, he had an ear-to-ear grin.

"Are you all right son?" his mother asked, as she could feel herself trembling.

"Great, Mom," he replied as he looked into the distance. "Dr. Addison really pulled that one out of the hat, didn't he? I can't go wrong with him on my side."

It was obvious that a situation that could have proven quite unnerving had, on the contrary, a very positive effect on Alex's demeanor. He was not the slightest bit intimidated by the sight of a human heart or the urgency of the code, but rather felt rejuvenated by his doctor's valiant save in the face of death.

The monorail ride to the hotel was spent in silence and the duo initially entered Jane's room. She phoned home and nervously detailed the day's events to her husband. After talking to the remainder of the family, Alex was allowed to choose a movie from the pay-per-view options in his own room. He kissed his mother good night as she tucked him in his bed, something she hadn't done in years.

The movie was just a distraction as Alex sat up in bed thinking of the day's developments and contemplating tomorrow's adventures. He placed his borrowed rosary beads on the nightstand and gingerly positioned Reggie Jackson on the pillow next to his own. Falling asleep was no great challenge as he was wiped out from both an emotional and physical standpoint. He pushed the "sleep" button on the remote control and was dreaming before the allotted fifteen minutes of viewing had expired.

His mother, on the other hand, was wide awake and staring at a blank television. She couldn't imagine what the parents must have been going through in that room today. From her vantage point, she was unable to see the action in room seven and her most vivid memory was of the parents being escorted from the room by a nurse's aide.

Although it had always been her contention not to feel sorry for herself or her children, she couldn't help but wonder why Alex was afflicted with such a condition and the thought of losing him made her stomach turn. He was such a precious child who had never harmed another soul and the vision of him being split open like a clam exaggerated the visceral responses she was already feeling.

Her fear turned to anger and she began questioning her faith. Why would a god make such a young child suffer? Why were any of the children at Ridgewood hospital suffering? What had they done to deserve any of the grief they were experiencing? There was no answer to be found in her room at the Ridgewood Hotel and she resigned herself to accepting the lack of sleep she would get that evening. She turned on the news and began to commiserate with the earthquake survivors who had lost loved ones in Bangladesh.

CHAPTER 4

The next day started as quietly as the previous night for Alex. He was one day away from being put to sleep, having his heart stopped, and having it fixed; the entire concept seemed beyond his imagination on the eve of his operation.

How could they stop an organ, work on it, and guarantee that it could be restarted? How many children, he wondered, actually had their chests reopened in the intensive care unit and how much would each remember of the event? These thoughts made him nauseous and starving for fresh air. The hotel alarm clock read 6:00 AM and since his mother would still be sleeping, he put on a sweatshirt and pants and made his way outside the hotel.

The Ridgewood facility prided itself on catering to children and this hotel was no exception; abutting the parking lot was a very elaborate park constructed entirely of wood. A small plaque at the park's entrance identified the McDonald's corporation as major contributors to its construction and this explained the large wooden clown carousel in the center. Given the hour, Alex thought he would have the facility to himself but was surprised to see another child sitting quietly on one end of the seesaw. The stranger appeared to be about his age although children with chronic illnesses predictably fell below the curve when it came to weight and height comparisons.

He quietly advanced across the park and assumed a position directly across from the other child. A dark-skinned boy with jet black hair and almond brown eyes slowly raised his eyes to meet Alex's as they exchanged smiles.

"Hi, my name is Alex, and I'm from Maine."

"Hello, my name is Nikhil and my friends call me 'Nicky'," the boy replied after a brief delay. His words were slightly slurred and he seemed to struggle to find exactly the right ones.

"Are you here with a relative or what, Nicky," Alex pursued. "I'm here to have an operation tomorrow. Ya see, I have a hole in my heart and sometimes I don't get enough oxygen, causing me to turn blue. Dr. Addison is my doctor and he saved a little boy's life yesterday. I'm only a little bit scared of the breathing tube and not waking up, and of comas and everything but I'm pretty sure it's gonna be fine. I plan to try out for shortstop next year. My dad's a heart surgeon but he doesn't do kids. I have a new baby brother. His name is Evan . . . " He had no idea why he was spewing out all this information but it seemed that Nicky was a great listener.

He was right. Nicky not only listened to Alex but was interested in what he was saying. Eventually he was afforded an opportunity to share his story and was able to tell it as only a child could.

"My name is Nicky Malhotra. My family is originally from India but now we live in Manhattan. My dad is an engineer and I have two sisters named Priya and Anjoo. I have a brain tumor on the left side of my head . . . First, I couldn't move my right arm and now I can't find the words I want to say. I am also going to have an operation tomorrow and I also think it will be fine. I am staying with my mother at the hotel and my sisters are at the neighbor's house back home. I don't like baseball but I play tennis and golf with my father." And just like that, the two boys were friends.

There was no need to discuss their illnesses any further as this was a time to play and relax before heading to the hospital. The seesaw was followed by the slides and eventually the sandbox. It was obvious that Nicky was limited in the use of his right arm and Alex unconsciously found himself helping out during climbs and with the larger toys. The boys bonded in a very short period of time.

"Alex, honey, it's time to get going."

Alex looked over his shoulder and saw his mother fully clothed and en route to the hospital. "I'm sorry, Nicky, but I can't play anymore," he said regretfully.

"That's okay, " Nicky stammered. " I'll see you later."

Alex and his mother had a quick breakfast at the hotel before boarding the monorail for the hospital. Although the weather had turned cloudy, his mood couldn't have been brighter. Today he would be meeting with Drs. French and Addison, his cardiologist and surgeon, respectively. A cardiac catheterization and echocardiogram were also slated for the day's activities.

A quick stop at the main reception desk preceded an elevator trip to the fourth floor. Dr. French was a very prominent cardiologist and had been following Alex's condition over the last few years. He was second in command behind Dr. Einthoven and was expected to replace him as chairman of the department in two years.

The Cardiology waiting area was decorated with a carnival theme and, unlike the blood drawing area, was quite pleasing to the eye. Amidst the carousels, roller coasters, and Ferris wheels were posters depicting the normal human heart and several with the more common anomalies. Alex identified the graphic delineating his lesion although it made no more sense to him than before. His mother looked over his shoulder and was able to explain the basics using her nursing background but the pathology remained confusing.

"Here is the hole between the left and right ventricles," she began, trying to keep it as basic as possible, "and this is the pulmonary artery connecting the right side of the heart to the lungs. Somewhere in this region a blockage prevents blood from entering the lungs and redirects it through the hole."

"That kinda makes sense, Mom. What do you think they are going to use to patch the hole?"

"It is a synthetic patch made of a clothlike material that the body will not reject. Based on my research, the patch will become incorporated into the heart as a lining of cells covers it."

Jane Harkins had spent numerous hours on the internet and browsing through her husband's textbooks in order to better understand Alex's condition. His congenital heart defect variant didn't always become symptomatic during the early years, which explained Alex's relatively late presentation. He had been fine as a child and although there was evidence of disease progression by echocardiogram, his cyanosis was a relatively new development.

"This must be Alex," said the nurse in Dr. French's office. "The doctor will see you now." Alex entered the examination room and was instructed to put on a hospital gown.

"Geez, I wonder why these things don't have any backs to them," he said to his mother, "I don't think there's anything wrong with my butt so why does it have to be flapping in the wind like this."

"You have a very cute little tushy, son. Be proud of it."

"Funny, Mom."

Dr. French entered the room after fifteen minutes and was wheeling a very large piece of equipment behind him. Alex had seen this contraption before and recognized it as the echocardiogram machine.

"Well, hello young man," Dr. French said enthusiastically. "It's been about six months hasn't it? You're looking well. Oh, by the way, have you bought that Porsche yet?"

Over the years they had discussed many topics unrelated to health care matters and Dr. French was also a sports-car buff. He was a very intelligent man and had the appearance of a true scholar. The lower half of his face was covered with a closely trimmed salt-and-pepper beard and half-frame wire-rim glasses sat on the tip of his nose. His hair was also a mix of black and white and Alex had always thought that if turned upside down, he would look exactly the same. His formal training was in Boston in one of the Harvard programs and it would've been an event to see him without his collegiate bowtie and sweater vest. Alex concluded that Dr. French and his grandfather shared the same tailor.

"Naw, Dr. French, I'm not sure I could reach the pedals yet. How is your little beauty?" He responded referring to the doctor's 911 Cabriolet.

"Great! In fact, I just took it out of storage. The sun's warming up which means the top's going down. Perhaps we can go for a short spin before you leave Hitchcock."

"That would be awesome," Alex shrieked as he practically jumped off the examination table. The day's events just kept getting better and better.

Dr. French proceeded with the physical exam. His stethoscope had a small stuffed elephant affixed to the bell and this aid proved to be an invaluable distraction during the examination of babies and young children. The scope glided across Alex's chest as the examiner remained emotionless. This humane quality was taught early in medical school in efforts to avoid alarming the patient should any pathology be detected.

"You know, Alex, your chest is like a big seashell and I'm confident these are ocean noises I'm hearing."

"Well, I do live on the beach, Dr. French," He answered without missing a beat. "But seriously, does it sound bad, sir?" his sarcasm had been toned down substantially as he became more comfortable with the situation.

"There's no doubt the murmur is more prominent and I've noted obvious changes in your nailbeds. That's okay; though, I mean, it was expected. The goal here was to have the surgery before irreversible damage has occurred. The hole between the chambers is an outlet for your right ventricle and once it's gone, your heart still has to be able to tolerate the increased workload. In other words, the time is definitely now."

Jane Harkins interjected, " We're right on course then, Dr. French?"

"You bet."

Alex was instructed to assume a supine position as clear gel was placed over his heart. The ultrasound transducer was placed to the left of his breastbone and felt fifteen degrees cooler than the stethoscope. Images came up immediately on the screen and were not remotely discernable to the uneducated eye. Alternating areas of gray and white static graced the monitor resembling a television tuned in to an unprogrammed channel.

"It's obvious, as you can see, folks," Dr. French began his explanation, "that there is a cold front coming from the southeast and heading to the mid-Atlantic states. This, up here, is the jet stream . . . " he paused for a response. His attempts at humor were greatly appreciated and all in the room expressed amusement.

"This is your right heart," he continued seriously, "and this is the ventricular-septal defect. Let me put some color on it," he stated, as he turned up the flow-velocity setting, "and it should become more obvious. This is the flow across the defect and it's clearly greater than your previous study. The red areas are the regions of greatest turbulence and these, too, have become more prominent from the time of your last echocardiogram. The heart catheterization later this afternoon will put the whole picture together for us."

"Sounds good, Dr. French," Alex and his mother uttered at the same time. Alex dressed himself as the two adults left the room. He and his mom were told that a two-hour delay awaited them before the angiogram and they decided to eat a late breakfast at the McDonald's downstairs.

As they descended on the elevators, it became readily apparent why these were such a hit with patients. An unobstructed view of the lobby was afforded to the rider similar to a gondola on a ski mountain. Children could be seen playing with stuffed animals strewn throughout the ground floor as coins were continually being tossed into the central fountain and, all the while, the red-haired clown pleasantly welcomed patients and their families into the corner restaurant. The designers of the hospital deserved a lot of credit, he thought, for turning this potentially morbid place into a pleasant and almost festive space.

They entered the restaurant and as Alex's turn came to place his order, he reviewed the overhead menu.

"May I help you, sir?" said the attentive food server.

"Yes, please," he said slowly as he was still going through the options. "I think I'll have a McSausage biscuit, a

McHashbrown, and some McOrange juice before my McHeart operation." This attempt at humor fell on deaf ears and the young girl behind the counter diligently went about collecting the items.

The pair ate breakfast in relative silence, each thinking about the morning's events. He asked if they could go visit the child from the code yesterday but his mom thought it inappropriate. To lighten the mood, he brought up Nicky Malhotra and went on to describe his neurologic deficits. Coincidentally, his mother had met Mrs. Malhotra at the hotel and they spent a fair amount of time discussing the upcoming surgeries.

"You know, Alex," his mother said cautiously, "Nicky has a very malignant tumor and his mother is quite concerned for him. I feel very lucky that we are not dealing with a cancer in your case and that your heart condition is treatable."

"Don't worry, Mom. I could tell by the look in Nicky's eyes that he knew everything is going to be fine. He didn't seem concerned at all. Some kids just know."

With this, the duo headed for the catheterization lab. It was located within the radiology department although the procedure would be performed by Dr. French, a cardiologist. Another registration was required and the wait seemed unbearable. The process had been explained to Alex on a previous visit and involved the insertion of special catheters designed to pass through and analyze his heart. This procedure seemed minor compared to the eventual operation and, although somewhat nervous, he maintained a poised front.

Alex was led into the catheterization suite by one of the technicians and the sight was overwhelmingly intimidating. The room was kept quite dim to facilitate visualization of the images after contrast injection and monitors were located at every corner, two of which recorded his vital signs during the procedure. The table was cold steel and a large C-shaped mechanical arm with a camera mounted at its tip straddled his midportion. Aprons containing lead shields hung from hooks along the wall and served to protect the physicians and technicians during periods of fluoroscopy.

"Do you have any allergies to shellfish?" the technician asked.

Alex thought this was a particularly strange question but responded, "Not that I know of, although I don't routinely eat seafood. Why do you ask?"

"There are some individuals with fish allergies that develop a reaction to the dye we use for this study. It's usually not a big deal but sometimes it can be. On occasion, people's faces swell up and breathing becomes difficult and if we know that beforehand, we can pre-medicate and decrease the likelihood of it happening."

The technician spoke in a somewhat aloof manner as he went about preparing the room for the procedure.

Methodically, several sterile packages were opened containing gowns, instruments, and catheters of various sizes. Concomitantly, several other technicians entered the room and began the gowning process while a nurse started an intravenous line in Alex's left arm.

Dr. French was paged to the cath lab as the final preparations were completed. He entered the room, greeted Alex again, and donned his lead. There would be no joking on this occasion. Although considered a relatively minor procedure, all catheterizations had the potential for complications and even death.

"Alex, I'm going to inject some lidocaine into your groin. This is the same stuff you get at the dentist's office that numbs your teeth. In a few minutes, you will still be able to feel pressure but shouldn't feel any pain where I am working. Here goes."

As he completed his sentence, Alex felt a sharp prick in his right groin. This caught him somewhat by surprise despite the warning and he reflexively jerked his leg off the table.

"I know it's tough Alex, but you've got to stay still. Give him a half milligram of Ativan and two of Versed," Dr. French ordered. These medications were meant to help Alex relax and almost as soon as they were ordered, a nurse had injected them into his peripheral IV. Initially he became a little lightheaded but eventually the sensation became quite pleasant as a feeling of profound relaxation and well-being overcame him. Thoughts of the catheterization left his mind and he began daydreaming about Mills Creek, the baseball team, and his sisters.

This relatively brief period of euphoria was abruptly interrupted by a feeling of deep pressure in the groin. The sensation traveled down the outside of his leg into his foot and his entire extremity felt temporarily paralyzed. Dr. French had accessed his femoral artery with a large-bore needle and had passed a wire through it; this discomfort coincided with the passage of a catheter into the aorta as it advanced toward *his* heart.

"Okay, Alex?"

He answered in the affirmative although this was clearly an uncomfortable feeling. Still somewhat dazed from his medications, he began to see images on the ceiling-mounted screen.

As the contrast was injected, pictures of his own beating heart appeared on the screen and the images seemed unreal. It was almost like watching a documentary on television and this easily could have been pictures of any patient, but it wasn't. The people in the room were watching *his* heart.

Although he had no medical basis to support his interpretation, the images just didn't seem right. Dr. French tried to explain the findings as they appeared on the monitor but the sedation precluded Alex from processing the information. The original catheter was replaced by one with a different angulation, over the same wire, and more shots were taken. At one point, his heart slowed to an unacceptably slow rate and Dr.

French ordered him to cough hoping this would result in a reflex increase in activity but Alex slowly began to fade as his mentation and blood pressure degenerated. Subsequently he developed a run of ventricular tachycardia and completely lost consciousness. It appeared the catheter had irritated his heart lining causing the malignant rhythm to develop.

"Get the code cart in the room and push one-hundred of lidocaine, stat," Dr. French stated, remaining outwardly calm. This complication was not unheard of during a catheterization and he felt somewhat reassured by the fact that there remained a blood pressure, albeit low, on the monitor and he could still feel a faint pulse.

As the dysrhythmia persisted, he proceeded to make a fist and pounded Alex across the breastbone. This maneuver had generally been abandoned with the advent of new medications but he was from the old school and it seemed appropriate at the time. Fortunately, Alex converted to a sinus rhythm and his pressure normalized. He regained consciousness and was completely oblivious regarding his eventful procedure.

Similarly, his mother remained unaware of the entire event as she sat in the waiting area. Dr. French thought there was no benefit in passing on the specific details to either of them as it would have no bearing on Alex's operation and would only prove worrisome to the already apprehensive parent. He secretly let out a sigh and was grateful for the rapid resolution of the problem. The remainder of the study was unremarkable and the information gained confirmed that there was no physiologic derangement present that would make the risks of surgery prohibitive.

Once he was sure that everything had stabilized, Dr. French attended to Alex's mother in the waiting area.

"Did everything go okay?" she asked, as she dropped the scraps of paper she'd been tearing for the last hour, "Is he all right? Did you find anything unexpected? Is the operation still on." Her questions were answered in the order they were presented.

"Yes, yes, no, and yes," Dr. French replied hoping to ease her tension with humor, "Just a little scare with his rhythm during the procedure. I think it would be in our best interest to keep him in the hospital overnight instead of the hotel. Look at it this way, the trip to the operating room tomorrow will be shorter than expected and there's less chance he'll try and make a break for it."

"You're scaring me doctor. This admission is purely precautionary, isn't it?"

"I assure you, Mrs. Harkins, Alex is fine. I think you, Alex, and I will all sleep better tonight if you stay in-house."

Dr. French's next job was to try in convince his patient to stay in a nonthreatening way. "Well, son," he began, "I have some bad news and some good news. Which do you want to hear first?"

"Bad," was the brief reply.

"The bad news is you don't get to stay in the hotel tonight. That's right, no pay-per-view movies, no candy on the pillow, and no free continental breakfast. On the bright side, McDonald's has a new kids meal and I believe a miniature replica of a Power Puff Girl is included. You can't beat that."

The small chuckle Alex offered made it clear that he had some understanding of the situation and would not prove resistant. "Fine, fine," he said, "but you've got to double the length of the Porsche ride."

"Deal."

After a few moments, an orderly transferred Alex's stretcher to the fourth floor children's ward. As he was wheeled through the unit he could see a number of children wandering aimlessly as if it were some morbid playground from a nuclear fallout. Three children were huddled at the far end of the hall wrapped in a myriad of bandages.

"Which one of those guys gets the fife and drum," Alex asked drolly, making reference to a painting he had seen depicting three tattered soldiers marching during the Revolutionary War.

"What the hell is a fife?" replied the uninterested orderly.

The ward was shaped like a rectangle and designed to

accommodate as many children as possible. Each room housed four patients and retractable curtains separated its interior into quadrants. Cribs alternated with hospital beds and children of all ages shared the floor.

At the end of the hall was a small space containing numerous toys, a picnic table, and a small indoor slide. This playground was off limits to adults and was dubbed Camp Ridgewood. Health care workers were also not allowed to enter the room and it was the closest a child could get to being away from the hospital without actually leaving the premises.

The nurse's stations contained all the requisite charts and vitals sheets stacked neatly in columns and the smallest children were left in strollers by this work space for observation as the nurses tended to other business. The television room behind the station contained several sets, some of which had attached video games. All in all, the fourth floor was not a bad place to spend a few days for a child despite its location within a hospital.

Alex's room had only one other occupant. A two-year-old Middle Eastern child peered through the rails of the crib resembling a caged animal observing a zoo employee. His mother was covered from head to toe in a long black outfit made of cotton and her face was covered in a veil leaving only her eyes visible. She bowed her head as the visitors entered the room as her custom deemed it unacceptable to make eye contact with strangers.

The two remaining slots contained hospital beds which were currently unoccupied. A small bathroom located in the corner served as a facility for the children and their parents; it was customary, and almost expected, that one member of the child's family stay overnight during the hospitalization. This was done for the comfort of the children and the nursing staff as misbehavior was easily curtailed with a parent in sight.

As Alex's mother entered the room, she glanced in the direction of his roommate and greeted the little boy's mother. Eye contact was established, because they were both females, and both parents exchanged caring and concerned glances. Empathy seemed to be a universal emotion free of cultural stigmas.

"Alex, this stay is a little bit unexpected and I'll have to return to the hotel in a bit to pack you a bag."

"I'll be fine, Mom," he said, trying to appear brave. "And please don't forget Mr. McKinley's gift and the travel chess set. I feel like beating up on Dad in a different state tonight."

His mother still wasn't completely convinced the catheterization proceeded without complication and the anxiety was clearly visible on her face. This unexpected twist caught her by surprise and her thoughts became somewhat clouded. Mark Harkins would be arriving at the airport in a few hours and arrangements would have to be made for his transport since she was not comfortable leaving Alex behind.

"You know what, Alex?" she began, her thoughts remaining distant, "I might as well get our stuff from the hotel now. It'll be one less thing to deal with later."

"Our stuff?" he questioned. "I have to stay in the hospital tonight, but you don't, Mom. I think you'll get a lot more rest in a comfortable bed at the inn." Alex was hoping she'd agree and although he wasn't trying to be overly courageous, he felt his mother would be a lot less fretful outside the hospital. His motives were not purely unselfish, as her apprehension was beginning to make him feel ill at ease.

"No fears, young man, we're in this together." With that she gathered her purse, kissed him on the forehead, and made her way toward the door.

"I will look after him for you while you are gone," whispered the other child's mother realizing that this would prove comforting to Alex's mom during her absence.

"Don't forget the chess set and Mr. McKinley's package, Mom." He wished his dad could arrive earlier but knew he had patients to attend to prior to leaving.

A nurse entered the room and introduced herself as Karen. "Hello, Alex, I'll be your nurse tonight. Let me know if there's anything I can get you during your stay."

This segueway seemed very much like a stewardess's speech at the beginning of a flight and he secretly hoped she would not ask him to raise the back of his bed for safety reasons.

"Do I still need this IV?"

"Actually, you don't. Let me convert it to a heplock and you'll be able to walk around the ward and meet some of the other children. I will have to put you on telemetry, however." She attached several leads to his chest and wrapped a portable EKG transducer around his neck. "This way, we'll be able to follow your heart rhythm as you're up and about."

Alex dragged himself out of bed and was still a little sore at the intravenous site. He motioned to the child's mother that he would be just outside in the hall should anyone come calling for him and she nodded her approval all the while avoiding eye contact.

At the nurse's station were two clerks and each appeared to be in their late teens. He was feeling quite gregarious, probably from nerves, and struck up a conversation with the one closest to him.

"So, do you work here?" was all he could muster. Fortunately he wasn't trying to pick her up at a club as this line was old and usually ineffective.

"Well, part time," she replied in a high-pitched voice. "I also go to school at the north Hancock campus. I'm studying ancient history."

Ancient history, Alex thought. Was there anyone studying *recent* history?

The young lady was quite attractive and was wearing a cutoff muscle shirt and hip-hugging blue jeans. This guise was further enhanced by her sequin pumps with six-inch heels. The look, he thought, would be considered overdressed for a prostitute in New York City and certainly looked out of place in a hospital.

"You must be Alex, our new admission."

Alex confirmed this and was somewhat taken aback by his name plate on the clerk's desk. It was official; he was here for his heart operation.

His next stop was Camp Ridgewood where he joined two children already at play. He introduced himself and after a few uncomfortable minutes, initiated a conversation.

"Hi, guys; I'm Alex Harkins from the great state of Maine." He found himself sounding like a beauty contestant during the interview phase of a pageant.

"Hi, Alex; my name is Josh. As you can see, I've recently had my left leg removed because it had a bad cancer. The doctors don't think it's spread yet but they're not sure." This utterance was said so matter-of-factly that it took Alex by surprise; only a child could summarize such a grave situation in two sentences. Josh had taken to wearing a black eye patch and Alex inquired if this was part of his therapy.

"No, not really. I know I'm going to be called 'peg leg' or 'Captain Bly' or something when I get my artificial leg so I might as well make the most of it. I've always wanted to be a pirate and my father bought it for me. I'm even practicing my expressions, you know, 'aye-matey' and 'scallywag' and all that." Alex and the other child laughed at Josh's weak attempt at piracy.

What an excellent idea, Alex thought, and Josh had shown incredible insight. Kids would invent all kinds of names for Josh as soon as he left Camp Ridgewood, but within its confines, his illness didn't matter. This really was a sanctuary for the kids and, unfortunately, their lives would have to be spent fighting reality on the outside.

The other child's name was Benjamin and he had been admitted for a heart transplant, which explained the surgical mask he was required to wear each time he ventured from his hospital room.

"I'm really from the fifth floor but I met Josh by the fountain a couple of weeks ago. It's boring to stay in your room all the time so my doctors let me visit a couple of hours a day. My heart's failing because it's really swollen and the medicines don't help anymore. Dr. Addison said they're trying to get me a new one but there are a lot of people waiting in line. I hope, when I do get one, it's from a little boy 'cause I don't want to start playing with dolls and all that sissy stuff." Again, a brief and unemotional description of a grave situation was offered. "What are you in for?"

This question could have easily been asked to a prisoner and in Benjamin's case this wasn't too far from the truth. He had been in the hospital for the last eleven months and had almost resigned to never leaving. What a terrible existence, Alex supposed, as he told them his story.

"You're lucky," Benjamin stated without making eye contact, "sounds like Addison's gonna be able to fix your heart and you'll be home soon." With that, it seemed he was no longer interested in establishing a friendship with Alex as he'd seen many other children leave the hospital and each good-bye was more painful than the last.

The children played a pirate game for Josh's benefit, followed by cowboys and Indians for Ben; the surgical mask he was wearing lent itself to a bank robber fantasy set in the Old West and Alex was more than happy to participate for Benjamin's benefit.

Soon enough it was time for the other children to receive their medications and the group dispersed as quickly as it had assembled. Josh wheeled himself back to his room and Ben left without saying good-bye. Alex was left at camp by himself and rather than feeling lonely or sorry for himself, he kneeled and thanked God for the care the boys were receiving and for the doctors who dealt with this kind of agony on a daily basis.

"Alex, you have a phone call," the receptionist informed him. "I think it's your mother."

"What, did you miss me already, Mom?" he answered sarcastically before saying hello.

"Actually it's Sandy, Alex. I got the number from your mother at the hotel. I didn't think you'd be spending tonight in the big house so I had a bunch of balloons sent over to your room at the inn."

"Oh man, Sandy, I mean that's so nice of you." This conversation, predictably, made his heart race, alarming the nurse responsible for his care. She burst into the room asking if everything was okay.

"Your heart rate just doubled on the monitor, Alex. Is anything wrong?"

He was tremendously embarrassed and cupped his hand over the speaker on the phone lest Sandy hear the nurse's statements.

"Just fine," he mouthed as he turned redder than his blood had ever been. "I guess the baby across the room just startled me a little bit." With this he received a sideways glance from the child's mother and eye contact was definite-ly established, indicating her disappointment with Alex's exaggeration of the truth.

"What's going on?" Sandy asked in a concerned voice.

"Aw geez, nothin'. These nurses make the biggest deal over nothin'. Must be her first day on the job." This additional falsification earned him a second glance from the covered one in the corner.

"Are you getting a bit nervous, Alex?"

He answered "no" although the response fell on deaf ears. He continued the dialogue by describing the children he had met in the playroom and their unfortunate illnesses. The conversation eventually ended as he thanked Sandy profusely for the phone call and balloons, and upon hanging up, the funny sensation in his knees returned helping him finally to realize its significance.

Alex's goofy and infatuated trance was interrupted by the sound of Dr. Addison's voice, which he recognized although the two had never formally met. He was a dark-skinned man with blue eyes and jet-black hair; in fact, his skin tone was almost bronze. Accompanying him were three medical students and a senior resident. The crew initially paused in front of Alex's roommate as the attending surgeon began his dissertation.

"Doctors," he began, much to the delight of the young medical students who were unaccustomed to the title, "this is baby Ahmed, our ASD repair from Monday. Who can tell me why we operate on these patients?" An overly eager female student raised her hand as if she were in the back row of a large auditorium and barely visible.

"Atrial septal defects come in three flavors, the most common of which is the secundum defect. With time, left uncorrected, these lesions can cause irreversible changes in the lungs' circulation and therefore they should be corrected before the age of three. I was there when you performed the operation, Dr. Addison, and it was the highlight of this rotation."

Oh give me a break, Alex thought. What a total brownnoser. He had half a mind to jokingly offer her a tissue so she could symbolically wipe the stool off her nose from being so far up Dr. Addison's colon. He knew the type; every class had one.

Dr. Addison was no fool and he had met a thousand students like her in the past. He responded sardonically, "That's correct, young lady, and I'm sure it was a highlight for you. As a matter of fact, have you seen any other operations this month?"

She shook her head from side to side and almost showed some remorse for her blatant attempt at being a kiss-ass.

"Anyway, the baby is doing fine and how are you, Mom?" he said, motioning to the child's parent.

"Well, Dr. Addison," came the response as the grateful

 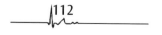

family member turned away, "Mohan is eating more now and slept throughout the night. I wish to thank you from the bottom of my soul." Although this wasn't the exact expression she was looking for, it did convey her gratitude and made Dr. Addison blush.

"Great, let's move on. Well, hello, young man. I'm Dr. Addison. You look a little too healthy to be in the hospital. Are you sure you're just not trying to mooch a few free meals from McDonald's at your parents' expense."

"I assure you that if I tried to run across the room, you may see a different side of me," Alex offered humbly. "My name is Alex Harkins and you will be operating on me tomorrow. I saw you save that boy's life in the intensive care unit yesterday but was too shy to introduce myself."

"Let's see. Alex . . . Alex. Oh yes, Mark Harkins little boy. What a pleasure to meet you. Your father and I go a long way back and I am absolutely honored he wants me to perform your operation."

"My dad's always said the biggest compliment you can pay a heart surgeon is to let him operate on a family member. He has all the confidence in the world in you, sir."

"Mark was quite a character you know, son," Dr. Addison continued as he developed a distant stare. "Man, he and I used to really chase the nurses. He had his eye on Renee, but I got to her first; I don't think he ever forgave me for that. He was quite a hound, though, and I have never seen so many girls come out of someone's call room . . . "

With this utterance he abruptly terminated his oration realizing this trip down memory lane was best taken with Alex's dad himself.

"I'm sorry, Alex; I hope you don't think I'm a complete goof for discussing our residency."

"Not at all, Dr. Addison; in fact, I'm glad to hear that Dad was a normal guy once upon a time. He's turned into quite a square." The entire assembly laughed aloud and Alex appreciated his doctor's ability to put him at ease.

"Now then, students," Dr. Addison continued, "Our patients here has a variation of Tetralogy of Fallot. As you know, this is one of the four most common congenital cyanotic heart defects and in Alex's case, it really didn't become worrisome until recently. I have three cases tomorrow and you should each scrub in on one."

"Boy, Dr. Addison, I'd really like to see that operation," chimed the overanxious butt-kisser.

"Yes, I suspected you might, Denise," he said, winking to his resident. "Alex, I hope to see your dad before the operation; we've got a lot of catching up to do." Upon finishing the sentence he turned toward the door and was flabbergasted to see Dr. Harkins as he entered the room.

"Well look at you, ya ol' fart. You always did have the worst timing, Harkins." The two men exchanged an embrace and shook hands vigorously. "Man it's good to see you," Dr. Addison continued, "and thank you for the opportunity to fix your son."

"Dave, you always did have the best hands in the group. Who else would I pick?"

He turned to his son and said excitedly, "How's it goin', Alex? I got the message from your mom on my beeper that you'd be staying here tonight so I came to the hospital directly."

"But Dad, I thought you were coming later this evening; it's great to see you."

"I canceled my last case for today and took an earlier flight. It wouldn't be fair to my patient to have his operation performed by a surgeon who can think of nothing but his son. I'm sure you don't want Dave here distracted during your surgery. Got a minute to talk?" he motioned to Dr. Addison.

"You bet, Mark. Students, why don't we meet in the neonatal intensive care unit in forty-five minutes. Dr. Harkins and I need to review some details." With this the two gentlemen stepped out of Alex's earshot and only parts of the conversation remained audible.

"Increased cyanotic spells . . . reconstruct right ventricular outflow tract . . . arrhythmia in the cath lab . . . "

It was not imperative that Alex hear the contents of the conversation as it was on a highly technical level. He was ecstatic that his dad would consider canceling an operation to be with him and, in his mind, there was no such thing as "too little, too late". After completing the conversation in the corridor, his father returned to the room with bag in hand.

"I think I'll stay with you here tonight, son. Your mother's a wreck and she could benefit from a good night's sleep at the hotel. I've already asked your nurse to bring a lounge chair for me and I think I'll post up between your bed and the window. I did promise your mother that I would meet her at the hotel, so let me break away for a few minutes to round her up. Well, actually the truth of the matter is, Alex, that I need an excuse to ride the monorail. It is pretty credible, don't you think."

"I figured you'd like that, Dad. That was your favorite part of our last trip to Disneyland. It was kinda pathetic, though, when you put your arms above your head as if it were a roller coaster or something. I mean, how embarrassing."

"Be back in a jif."

His father left the room and Alex settled into bed as the day had been draining on this, the eve of his operation. As he began to think of the morning's events, a nurse entered the room carrying a plastic bag of clothes and an IV pump.

"Looks like you're going to get a roommate, young man," she said, while preparing the bed next to his." In fact, the inn's gonna be full tonight."

Alex glanced at the bag containing clothes and they appeared to belong to a child about his size. Before he knew it another patient and his mother entered the hospital room.

"Hello, Alex, my mother always says friends meet again if they want to."

It was Nicky! Alex couldn't have asked for a more pleasant surprise and practically jumped from his bed at the sight.

"Oh man, Nicky, it's awesome to see you again. What the hell are you doin' in my room anyway? That's right, you're going to the OR tomorrow too. Tonight's gonna be like a sleep over, ain't it?"

"I guess so, Alex, if your idea of a sleep over is having large needles stuck in your arms and having parents at the bedside. You have quite the party mentality." Alex didn't realize Nikhil possessed such a dry sense of humor and this aspect of his personality endeared him even more.

"That's true. All right, so it's not summer camp, but it beats staring at the ceiling or at Brun Helga the human bloodsucker." This reference eluded Nicky as his bloodwork had been performed at an outlying institution.

"Hello, Alex, my name is Seera Malhotra and I am Nikhil's mom. He hasn't stopped talking about you since the playground; you've left quite an impression. By the way, will your mother be joining you here tonight? I had the pleasure of meeting her earlier at the hotel."

"Yes, ma'am, she and my father will be returning shortly. It's great to see Nicky again."

"Would you be interested in joining us for a snack at McDonald's, Alex?"

He was more than happy to assent and the trio headed downstairs for a bite. It was Nikhil's first time staying in the hospital and Alex gave him the grand tour which included pressing the fire alarm on the elevator to pause it between floors. "It's the only way to appreciate the view, Nicky," he said, much to the chagrin of Mrs. Malhotra.

Alex's parents were waiting in the room as they returned and his dad quipped, "I thought you made a break for it, son. I fully expected to see your face on the back of a milk carton on my next trip to the grocery store."

"Yeah, maybe you'd see both our faces on those cartons, Dad, except Nicky's would have to be on a chocolate milk container," Alex joked, referring to his friend's dark complexion. After a group laugh, introductions were in order and Alex was the master of ceremonies. As the boys settled in, his father challenged them to a game of chess while the mothers broke off to commiserate.

"I'm very worried about Nicky, Mrs. Harkins. His neurosurgeon reviewed the films with us today and expressed some concern about his ability to resect the tumor safely. He was afraid that it may prove to be too invasive and attempts at cure could be dangerous. My heart sank when I heard this."

"I can't imagine what you're going through," Alex's mother replied. "I mean, what could possibly be going through your head realizing that beautiful child has a brain tumor? And please, call me Jane."

"Thank you, Jane. I am Seera; and I'm also petrified. How are you dealing with Alex's upcoming operation?"

"Poorly. I'm finding complete denial to be a good coping mechanism." Both women allowed themselves to laugh nervously as they turned their gazes to their respective children. "Unfortunately, my husband's taking it even worse than I, although you wouldn't guess that by looking at him."

The three boys were engrossed in a game of chess and Alex had no problem beating both his opponents handily. Nicky excused himself from the competition stating he was feeling a bit worn but in reality was experiencing a migraine headache resulting from the swelling around his tumor. The only means of palliation he found successful was assuming a recumbent position with eyes shut, although this was becoming less effective in the past few weeks. As she watched her son break from the group and isolate himself, Mrs. Malhotra realized what was happening and rushed to her son's side.

"Nickou, ap ko pain medicine chaya," she said in quiet Hindi.

"Hungee, Mommy, bothi durd hoora ha." The pain was significant and he requested analgesics.

Alex's family spent the next two hours together reminiscing and making phone calls to his sisters at home. His grandfather offered a final few words of unsolicited advice, the thrust of which was not to let the anesthetic turn him into a twit like his uncle.

After much deliberation, his mother agreed to stay in the hotel overnight and let the boys remain in the hospital. A tearful good-bye preceded her departure and releasing Alex from her embrace was almost unbearable; she uttered "I love you" and "my little boy" repeatedly as she clutched his head in her bosom and swung gently back and forth.

"One more day, baby, it's almost over," she whispered as she passed through the door making a conscious effort not to look back realizing this would open the floodgates of emotion once again. Alex felt a little lonely as her silhouette disappeared from sight, although he was not alone and this distinction became obvious to him for the first time.

Mrs. Malhotra had also assumed residence in a lounge chair next to Nicky and began unpacking her overnight bag. Her son was much improved after receiving a very strong narcotic and once again began to mill around the room. Mrs. Ahmed had retired for the evening and had drawn the curtains surrounding her child's crib after saying good night to the other families.

Alex and his father played yet another chess match when the final inhabitant of room 4124 was wheeled in; Alex's newest roommate was a four-year-old boy who was unresponsive and strapped in the seated position within his wheelchair. After introductions, an explanation was offered by his mother and it appeared young David had suffered a head injury after being struck by a motor vehicle at the age of two, which resulted in a permanent coma with no hope of recovery.

Alex and Nicky were taken aback by the sight as the limp body was transferred gently from chair to bed by the mother and nurse. The spectacle was eerie as the child stared blankly at the ceiling with a face totally devoid of emotion. In efforts to make David more comfortable, his arm and leg splints were removed and his extremities naturally postured in an inhuman position. A tracheostomy connected him to the ventilator as spontaneous ventilation was no longer possible and a clogged feeding tube was visible as it exited his stomach. The purpose of this admission, apparently, was to replace David's jejunostomy tube.

David's mother was diligent in her attentiveness to him and alternated placing saline drops in his eyes with wiping the saliva from the corner of his mouth as it ran almost continuously. She continued her story and was very forthright in admitting that the doctors had given her the option to withdraw support after the accident realizing the prognosis was so poor, but she couldn't bring herself to "kill" her little baby. Her attitude was quite realistic, however, and she realized that this level of function would be the highest he could attain and her life would be devoted to his care indefinitely. It was almost a calling, she explained, similar to those described by members of the clergy.

The child's image helped Alex and Nicky find a new sense of empathy. David would never go to the playground, have a first day of school, talk about a girlfriend, attend a prom, or visit home from college. His life would be spent at institutions as his mother grew old nursing him as her own life slipped away without ceremony. The sadness in David's eyes was reflected in his mother's as the two were inseparable throughout the evening.

"Please don't let me live like that, Mom," Nikhil whispered, realizing his surgery could leave him similarly incapacitated. "Promise you will let me go if I can't be like the other kids. I would never want you to spend your life in the hospital." This statement symbolized Nicky's unselfishness and his mother knew he was more worried for his family than himself.

"Oh Nicky, please don't talk like that," his mother replied, although the neurosurgeon had already addressed this potential complication. "Just pray to Bhagwan and things will work out. He has a master plan for all of us and I can't believe yours ends like this."

The hour was getting late and the nurse made her rounds

distributing medications and resetting the intravenous pumps. Alex's father and Mrs. Malhotra fell asleep without effort as the two boys lay awake; both agreed without significant deliberation that their time would be better spent playing video games in the TV room. With this they donned their hospital robes and slippers and headed into the hall. Upon approaching the viewing room they were stopped by the head nurse who asked, "Where are you boys headed, exactly?"

"Neither one of us can sleep because we are nervous about our operations," Alex volunteered without consulting Nicky, "and we thought a little time out here may tire us."

The nurse, against her better judgment, acquiesced but cautioned the children that if they were not back in their rooms in thirty minutes, their collective butts would be in a sling. The boys agreed without negotiation and were somewhat surprised that she permitted this clear violation of floor rules.

The TV room contained four sets, two of which had attached video bases. The pair sorted through the donated selection of games as if flipping through a card catalog using the Dewey decimal system before Nicky found one he liked.

"Hey . . . Alex," he struggled to say as talking became infinitely more difficult after a migraine, "here's an oldie but a goodie, 'Asteroids'. I've heard this has been around forever, let's give it a crack."

"Crack . . . Asteroids . . . crack, don't you mean hemorrhoids Nicky" Alex responded, proud of his play on words.

"Funny, Alex, you sound like my dad and no one laughs at him either."

The boys sat next to each other, knees bent, and gazed directly into the television like two Muslims at prayer. They alternated destroying the wayward asteroids approaching the triangular spaceship and tried to best one another game after game. Without establishing eye contact Nicky asked, "What did you think of David?"

"Breaks my heart-not that it's not a little broken already," Alex responded, but realized that this wasn't the time for humor. "I wonder if he can think straight and is unable to let anyone know; it would be like being trapped in a body for an entire life." With this, Alex had a flashback to the dream he had earlier in the week and was eager to terminate the conversation.

"I wouldn't want to find out," Nicky said pensively. "What do you think happens to you after you die?"

"You go to heaven," He answered matter-of-factly, "at least that's what I've been told."

"What do you think heaven is like?"

"It's high up in the sky and everything is white," Alex continued knowingly as if he had visited there on his last vacation. "You can't see the ground because of the clouds, kinda like an old-fashioned disco. Everyone is wearing a white gown made of cotton. In heaven you get to meet all your relatives who've died in the past and can talk for hours at a time because no one ever sleeps. Every day is like Christmas and you get just about everything you want if you ask God nicely and stay well mannered. The catch is, though, that not everyone can get in; you have to take a test at the gates made of pearl and if you fail you go directly to hell without passing 'GO'."

This Monopoly reference eluded Nicky and he continued to contemplate life after death. He gave Alex's description of the eternal resting place some consideration before describing his own interpretation of the hereafter.

"My family believes in something a little different," he began as his gaze became distant. "We believe in a place called nirvana. I suppose it's like your heaven and they're probably right next to each other in the sky, but everyone doesn't go to nirvana right away. My religion believes that once you die, you become born again either as another person or an animal or something. When my uncle Ravi died, my mother said he would probably come back as a Hindu priest because he was such a kind and gentle person during his life and this would be his reward. Good priests usually go on to nirvana but I think anybody can, if they're really nice to people." Nicky checked his peripheral vision to see if his new friend was even remotely interested in his explanation and was happy to see that Alex had stopped playing the game and had donated his undivided attention to the topic.

"It works both ways, though," he continued. "If Bhagwan gives you a lot during your lifetime and you abuse the privilege by being mean and selfish, you come back as a lesser person or animal in the next life. Our next door neighbor in Manhattan, Mr. Chattan, was very rich but also very mean, so when he passed away I thought he would come back as a rat or a flea or something until he redeemed himself. My mom calls the whole process reincarnation and that's why she believes that although friends go away or die, they'll probably be seen again in another person or animal later in life."

"I always thought of nirvana as a rock group with a dead lead singer but, anyways, what do you think it's really like up there, Nicky?"

"Like I said, it's probably a lot like heaven. Ya know, clouds instead of floors, all the people you'd want to meet milling around, and sunlight all the time. But I suspect the ladies would be wearing saris and the men dhotis instead of white gowns. I also think you can look down from nirvana and see what's going on down here on earth and that way, you can stay in touch and look out for your family."

"That's kind of an awesome concept, Nicky. I bet it keeps you on the straight and narrow as you go through life. I mean, one slip up and you're a fly with a bad attitude until further notice."

"I guess, Alex; I've never thought of it like that."

"And I bet you think twice before you squish a spider on the sidewalk. After all, it may be your long lost Uncle Abdul or something."

"If I didn't know better," Nicky said as he established formal eye contact with his flippant friend, "I'd think you were mocking me or something."

"Naw, don't take it so seriously little Nicky. I think your concept of death is excellent. Hey, and you know what, I just came up with a joke."

"I'm afraid to hear it but go ahead."

"Well, with your brain tumor and everything, I was just wondering what was *on your mind* tonight."

"Once again my little ashen friend," Nicky responded cynically, "no one laughs at my father either."

The brief reprieve from the serious tone of the evening was short-lived as the nurse in charge confronted the children and reminded them of their curfew. They restated their appreciation for the time allowed and headed to bed.

Mrs. Malhotra and Alex's father were fast asleep on the lounge chair adjacent to their respective beds and Mrs. Ahmed and David's mother had also called it a night. The stillness of the hospital was unnerving as was the intermittent clatter of young David's ventilator. The two boys slipped under their covers although neither was ready to call it a night; the next hour was spent in quiet conversation as the pair discussed plans for recovery and returning home.

Alex remembered Mr. McKinley's gift and took it from his father's bag. It was a small red box with a yellow ribbon and its card read "For Alex on the eve of his surgery".

"What's that?"

"Oh, it's just a little gift from the man who owns the country store back home. He's a great guy and he made me promise I wouldn't open the package till tonight."

With that he unraveled the bow and quietly opened the box. Enclosed within was another note which read,

Dear Alex, I suppose you're opening this the night before your operation and I want you to know I am praying for you. I gave this pendant to my lovely wife on our first date and she wore it until the day she died. I have kept it on a chain around my neck since that day, until now. It has brought me a world of Irish good fortune and I'd like to share it with you on this occasion. May the Luck of the Irish be with you.

Within the crumbled white tissue paper Alex found a gold four-leaf clover with the inscription, "To Margaret Mary, in the middle of a clover is love". With the rosary beads, the Reggie

Jackson baseball card, and the clover, he felt he was invincible and wished he could share this confidence with Nicky.

"Hey Nicky, do you believe in good luck charms?"

"I'm very superstitious, Alex, that's why I've worn this necklace with Lord Krishna on it since I was a child," Nicky responded flashing him a gold pendant dangling from a chain around his neck.

"Well, how about a lucky pair of rosary beads from my teacher? She said that they would bring me all the luck I needed and I'd like to share them with you even if you're not Catholic." Alex knew Sister Agatha would understand.

"That is very generous of you," Nicky said as he took his own charm off, "but it would be wrong if I didn't reciprocate." The two boys exchanged good luck pieces and this sectarian exchange could only be possible between children. Alex put Lord Krishna around his neck as Nicky wrapped the rosary beads around his wrist.

The banter eventually became forced as the boys realized the magnitude of the evening as they sat awaiting their respective operations. Nikhil stared across the room at the myriad of intravenous infusion pumps suspended at varying heights on metal poles as they illuminated young David's forehead. From a distance, the sight was almost pretty and reminded him of the Manhattan skyline as viewed from Queens.

"Alex, have you ever been to New York?"

"Naw," responded Alex as his somnolence became overwhelming, "but my parents were robbed once."

"Funny. When we get out of here I'm sure you could stay with us if you'd like. We could see some shows and museums and go to the top of the Empire State Building, or whatever. Maybe we could see a Yankees or Mets game; I know you'd like that. I can't wait."

"Sounds great, Nicky, just great."

CHAPTER 5

The sun shone through the slits in the dusty horizontal blinds as it cast an eerie shadow on the wall of Alex's hospital room. He sat up in bed and studied his surroundings. His father was not at his bedside; Nikhil and his mother had left for surgery; the Ahmeds remained behind a curtain of secrecy; and the lifeless David was attached to his ventilator as he remained motionless. This was definitely not Alex's bedroom.

After rubbing the sleep out of his eyes the magnitude of the moment hit Alex and he could feel his heart racing. This was the day and in a few hours his heart would be stopped and he'd be supported by a machine like his unfortunate roommate. The anxiety turned somatic as he felt his hands tremble while reaching for the water on his nightstand.

Why weren't his mother and father in the room? he wondered, and felt like crying but realized that an eleven year old was not expected to do so. Fighting back the emotions, he slipped on his moccasins and headed toward the door but prior to reaching the exit ran into his parents. Alex's mother grabbed him in a bear hug as she broke into tears.

"Jesus, mom," he choked, "I'm worried enough about not being able to breathe during this whole thing, can you let me up for a little air." His comments were ignored as the grip became even tighter and Alex's cheek moist from the crying.

"Okay, honey, the kid's got enough problems with turning blue already without your grip of death. Maybe let up a little bit and let a couple red blood cells go through his lungs." His mother broke the embrace and Alex was immediately in the arms of his father.

"I see," his mother said cynically, "I guess somebody has his own agenda. Try and leave a little squeezin' for me, will ya."

"Hey, where were you guys anyway."

"Your mother and I had a quick bite downstairs, son." This reminder sent a pang of hunger through Alex's body as he was instructed not to eat for twelve hours before surgery.

"Sure, rub it in. Why don't you go ahead and describe your meal so I can suffer even further. Fortunately, you probably ate at the McDonald's and that doesn't qualify as real food anyway."

"I'm sorry; I totally forgot about your food restrictions but don't worry, you'll be eating all those Mcmeat substitutes before you know it." His mother was swooning over him and was still chastising herself for not spending the evening at his bedside.

Alex's nurse entered the room and informed the group that transport personnel would be arriving soon. This announcement carried with it a certain sense of finality and the moment of truth was upon them. Both parents grabbed an extremity as if to ward off individuals entertaining the idea of taking their baby away but released their grasp upon realizing how ridiculous they appeared.

"Guys, you're embarrassing me," Alex stated calmly as apparently he was the only one who had come to terms with the situation at hand. He almost felt parental in his efforts to ease his parents' anxiety, "I think I'll go put on my hospital gown and moon people on my way to the OR."

The thought of Alex pressing his buttocks on the windows of the glass elevator as it descended and a lobby full of onlookers watching the Harkin's moonset made his father laugh aloud, drawing stares from others in the room.

"Look what Nicky gave me, guys. It's supposed to be a depiction of the Lord Krishna Kristofferson or something and it's brought him a ton of luck over the years. I traded Sister

Agatha's rosary beads for it although I don't get it, the person on this pendant isn't covered with a lot of body hair as far as I can tell."

"Alex, I hope you outgrow this stage of lunacy," his dad chastised, "it's not a hairy Krishna but rather the expression is Hara Krishna. I hope you didn't insult that young boy when he gifted you with his possession."

"Dad, we're buddies, and I was invited to visit his family in New York when this whole disaster is over."

The squeaks of a hospital stretcher could be heard as an orderly made the corner to Alex's room.

"All aboard," the jovial orderly dressed in white announced upon entering the room, "it's time for the nine A.M. Joey train with stops at the men's room, the gift shop, and the station at the operating room."

"Geez, Joey," Alex responded, "if that outfit was any whiter I'd think you were a tooth. At least offer me an ice cream or somethin', Mr. Goodbar."

"Yeah, well maybe I'll just run over you with my little ice cream stretcher, you little vanilla half pint." Joey's retort came without pause and this little hint of levity was appreciated by all in the room.

"Well, at least the boy's still got his sense of humor during all this, Joey," his mother interjected. "Just give us a minute to pack him a lunch."

Alex gathered his baseball card, newfound pendant, and four-leaf clover and tucked them within a pocket of his gown. He boarded the stretcher and covered his legs with a blanket lest his butt be exposed to the elements. He stared at David for a final time as he left and this reminded him how fortunate he was to have such a good prognosis. A glance at baby Ahmed playing in the crib as his mother slept faithfully at his bedside helped to reinforce this feeling of well-being as he realized he was the central thought of many individuals on that given morning.

The stretcher made the turn heading past the nurse's station and Camp Ridgewood on its way to the elevators. The trip was intentionally made in silence as Alex had put on his game face in preparation for the operation. He assumed a reclined position and attempted to relax as Joey inexplicably broke into a medley of songs from the Wizard of Oz.

"Great," Alex muttered, "I suppose I'm the one looking for a heart."

"I heard that, you little mutt," chimed the merry transporter. "I'd think you'd be the one looking for a brain." A throaty laugh followed as Joey had amused himself.

The fluorescent lights overhead passed like the dividing line on a highway and the assembly eventually boarded the elevators. The lobby seemed especially empty this morning as there was a paucity of visitors milling about at this hour. The entire atrium seemed less festive on this passage to the operating suite and even the clown in the corner seemed to have a sad expression.

"Listen, Joey," Alex begged. "I'll give you an original Reggie Jackson baseball card if you stop on the first floor for some breakfast. I'm starvin' and the warden back there on cell block four's been keeping me hungry for like a week."

"Gee, that sounds kinda temptin', young fella, but I'd lose my job if I did that."

"Did I mention the card was signed?"

"Oh, well, that changes everything. Let me just call my wife first and explain to her why I was fired today for feedin' a preop." In the short time he had spent with Joey, Alex could tell they shared a wry sense of humor and he wished they had met earlier.

"Did you take my friend Nikhil for his operation this morning, Joey?"

"You bet; he's already in the operating room. In fact, I think he's in OR nine, which is the one right next to yours."

After what seemed like an eternity the stretcher made its way to the preoperative waiting area and this room was reserved for patients and their immediate families as they awaited surgery. Multiple beds were strewn along the periphery of the room and curtains separated each cubicle, although none of them was drawn; parents found solace in spending the final moments before surgery with others in the same situation and the children found comfort in the bravery of those around them pending the same fate.

Alex and his parents became situated in cubicle seven and on either side were infants apparently awaiting cleft-lip surgery. He forced himself not to stare and expected the same from others.

His gaze was interrupted by a young nurse carrying an intravenous tray.

"Brun Helga," Alex spoke reflexively. "I mean, it's you again."

No one understood the reference but the nurse introduced herself as Heidi and confirmed that they had met before in preoperative testing. She was responsible for starting new IV lines in the holding area and asked Alex to stay still, once again reminding him he'd feel a small prick.

Alex remembered the last occasion when he had this procedure and sarcastically commented, "You know, I think I felt less of a prick when I was circumcised as a baby."

"That's enough, young man," his mother interrupted as

she felt his level of cynicism increasing. His mockery was almost like a barometer and one could gauge the level of anxiety based on his snide comments.

Dr. Addison was between cases and stopped by to check on Alex's status. "Well, hello, young man. We meet again. We're just about done turning the room over and we'll have you back there in a jif."

"No hurry," Alex commented under his breath.

"I'm Dr. Addison," he said, embarrassed to be stating the obvious as he introduced himself to Jane Harkins. "Listen, Mark, I think this is going to be relatively straightforward. The whole thing shouldn't take more than four hours and I'll come find you after I'm done. I promise you he'll be treated like my own son."

These words proved incredibly reassuring to the entire Harkin family even though they realized Dr. Addison was childless and single as a slice of processed cheese.

"Thanks David. You can imagine we're all a little uptight about this whole thing right now. You're probably like me a little bit-when I operate on someone it seems like a job but when it's a family member . . . anyway, I have all the confidence in the world in you."

"Enough said. I'll inform the room that we're ready out here and that should get the proverbial ball rolling."

"Dr. Addison," Alex interrupted, "my friend gave me this pendant. Can I wear it during the surgery?"

"Not around your neck because I'll be working there, but I promise you can when you wake up."

"Do you know how Nicky's operation is going?"

"Nicky?"

"Yes, Nicky Malhotra. He's slated to have an operation on his brain by Dr. Turcica."

"Sella Turcica?"

"Yes, I think that's it."

"I know the operation is under way in room nine, but I don't know what stage they're at." Dr. Addison intentionally lied for Alex's benefit; Nikhil's operation was being performed in the room next to his and there was a significant amount of commotion surrounding the procedure. Dr. Turcica had encountered unexpected bleeding during the dissection and repeated "stat" pages could be heard overhead for one of his partners. He knew the operation wasn't going well and could think of no benefit in informing Alex of the situation at the current time.

A second nurse informed the family that Alex would be transported to the operating suite in a matter of minutes. His mother began crying hysterically and drew the curtains around her.

"Alex, you're our pride and joy. Let's get this damn thing fixed and get home to the family."

"I'm with you, Mom. In fact, I am prepared to leave right now."

"Not so fast, young man," his dad interjected as he held back a combination of laughter and tears. "I'm getting a little tired of having Casper as a son. Let's get some red back into you and be done with it once and for all. We'll be praying for you, son, and, by the way, I have a little surprise for you when we get back home."

"What surprise?"

"You'll see when you get home; now give us both a monster hug."

The family embraced in unison and Alex found himself getting quite emotional. There was a ruffling behind the curtains and someone said, "Alex, are you back there?"

It was Mrs. Malhotra and she had come to wish Alex well. Her face was a pale white and she had obviously been crying.

"How's Nicky," he asked, but was afraid to hear the answer.

"Great, the operation is well under way. I just wanted to wish you and your family well before you headed back there and to let it be known that you were the last thing Nicky talked about before they put him to sleep. You've left quite an impression on him in the short time you've spent together and he insisted I invite you to our apartment in Manhattan this summer. So, consider yourself invited and we'll work out the details before you kids leave the hospital."

"That's so nice of you to offer," Alex's mother said as she wiped the tears off her cheeks, "and we'll be sure to reciprocate. Nicky seems like a fine boy and Alex would love to have him visit Maine as soon as he's better."

"Look, Mrs. Malhotra. Look what Nicky gave me last night."

She clasped the pendant in her hand as it dangled from Alex's neck, "You know, Nickou has had this on him since he was two years old. It was blessed at a temple in India by his grandmother before she died. He never parts with it and I don't think I've ever seen him take it off. He really must think a lot of you to pass it on."

"I guess so. He said it would bring me luck. It's Lord Krishna, right?"

"Yes, Alex, it is Lord Krishna, and yes it will bring you luck. On that very pleasant note let me leave you to spend time with your parents. I will be praying for you and we'll meet again in the PICU."

As Mrs. Malhotra departed an orderly came to transport Alex. The family said final good-byes and the stretcher left for the operating suite. His mother and father were directed to the waiting area but chose to visit the chapel first.

"It's in God's hands now, Mark, and I hope he guides David this morning."

"He will."

Alex entered the operating room and was greeted by several nurses and technicians. The room itself was quite large and devoid of windows in efforts to prevent potential contamination and the artificial light was so bright he was forced to cover his eyes from the glare.

"Hello, Alex," several people chimed in unison. He thought it quite unfair that they were allowed to wear operating masks and caps whereas he was completely uncovered. Nevertheless, there was an honesty in the room's occupants that was readily apparent in their eyes, a look of general concern and thoughtfulness. Amazingly, he didn't feel nervous in their presence and the whole process seemed almost routine and, in fact, almost too comfortable. The worker bees around him efficiently went about their business as the suite was prepared for the operation. He felt almost like a third wheel, as if he were intruding on their daily regimen like a relative invited to a birthday party as a formality.

The room was full of machinery and the display of technology was awe inspiring. Monitors mounted overhead were illuminated in neon colors and were flanked by large sets of lights resembling those at an outdoor sporting event. The ventilator stood guard at the cephalad end of the table and protected the anesthesiologist like a personal bodyguard.

Across from the entryway was a very intimidating machine housed in shiny steel and glass. Alex recognized this as the heart-lung machine and was humbled by the fact that it would support his life for several hours during the operation. His stare caught the attention of a burly man who barely fit into the scrubs assigned to him.

"Hello, young fella, my name is Turk and I'm the perfusionist. I'll be running this little beauty right here while they're working on your heart. I saw you staring at it so I don't think you'll mind a quick three-hour tour." The "Gilligan's Island" reference caught Alex by surprise and he couldn't help but think he was talking to the Skipper himself, given the man's size and naval tattoos plastered on his forearms.

"Yep, it's a Steimler special; four roller pumps cast in silver, a separate circuit for the cardiotomy suction, a top-of-the-line heat exchanger, and the finest membrane oxygenator money can buy. Oh man, this baby will take your flow from zero to 4 liters a minute in twenty seconds flat. Heck, if I wasn't married, I'd be courting this little baby myself."

"Oh my god," Alex said at a level only audible to himself,

"my life's gonna depend on Gomer Pyle while my heart's arrested."

"Sounds great, Turk," he said raising his voice, "but I think I'll wait for the turbo version before actually purchasing one."

"Heh, heh, heh," Turk drolled. "Did you here that, Rufus? The boy said 'turbo version'. I've got to remember that."

"Rufus," Alex exclaimed. "Jesus, I'm in Mayberry waitin' for Aunt Bea to call me in for apple pie. Hey guys, what happens if the power goes out while I'm on the heart-lung machine, is there a battery backup?"

"Naw, batteries are too unreliable. See that fifth chamber at the end of the machine, Alex?" Turk said motioning across the room, "that houses the Ridgewood cardiothoracic gerbil and energy wheel. That will keep you going if the lights go out, right, Rufus?"

"Enough, boys," Dr. Addison interrupted. "I think this would be a good time to gain Alex's confidence, don't you?"

"Yes, sir," both perfusionists replied embarrassingly.

Alex could only see Dr. Addison's eyes on this occasion but that was enough as the man exuded confidence and immediately put him at ease.

"All right folks, let's get this show on the road. Alex here is a special friend of mine and I don't want any more high jinx. Is that clear?"

The mandate came down like a ruling from a circuit court judge. Everyone in the room returned to their chores without question and were afraid to make eye contact with the disgruntled surgeon.

"C'mon Turk, let's get our patient onto the operating table."

"Alex, I make it customary for the patient to choose the music we play in the background as they go to sleep," Dr. Addison suggested. "Do you have any particular preferences?"

"Well, I guess we should pick something appropriate for the moment, sir, perhaps Bryan Adams' "Cuts Like a Knife" or "I've Got the Blues" by Cole Porter."

"You know, you remind me a lot of your dad, Alex-always quick with the jokes and one-liners. Unfortunately, on this occasion you just blew your right to choose and will have to listen to my selections. Let's see, perhaps "The Best of Minnie Pearl" or, "Yanni Plays the Acropolis and Loses," or my personal favorite, "Boxcar Willie Sings the Best of Burl Ives"."

"You've got to be kiddin' me, Dr. Addison."

"You're in luck, I am kidding. Maybe we'll just play a little bit of classical music, how's that? Maybe a little Beethoven, Mozart, or Bach."

"Actually, Dr. Addison, my dad told me last night that there was no *turnin' Bach* now."

"Good God man, did your old man pass on the gene for bad puns intentionally or are you being punished for something?"

"I'm sorry, sir; I get a little punchy when I'm nervous."

"No problem, lad; it's almost like I'm spending time with your father as a youngster when I hear your comments."

Hearing the word "lad" made Alex think of his grandfather. He knew the whole family would be thinking of and praying for him this morning and this gave him newfound strength as the final act was unfolding. He felt the cold steel of the operating table under his back as they tucked his arms at his sides with rolled blankets. The anesthesiologist had been setting up his equipment at the head of the table and finally introduced himself.

"Good morning, Alex. I'm Dr. Billings and I'll be your anesthesiologist for the operation. I tried to stop by and visit with you last night to answer questions but it seemed you and your roommate were not home at the time."

"You know Nicky, Dr. Billings? How is he doing? I know he's been in surgery for a while."

"I don't exactly know, son, but I'm sure he's doing fine. In any case, let's concentrate on your procedure. In a few minutes I'll be giving you some intravenous medications that will make you feel sleepy. Don't fight the urge to snooze, the goal is to keep you as comfortable as possible. There, I've injected some Versed and it will be taking effect almost immediately. Are you feeling a bit out of it?"

"Yes, sir, actually it feels pretty good and I'm not nervous at all. Thank you for keeping me comfortable. I was pretty scared last night and this morning."

"That's totally expected Alex, this is open-heart surgery you're having. If it makes you feel any better, Dr. Addison performed an operation on my little boy and he's doing just great. I have all the confidence in the world in his skills."

"Thank you, it is reassuring. Dr. Billings, I won't end up in a coma like David will I?"

"I don't know who you're talking about but the answer is an emphatic no. You have my word, son. I don't want that to be the last thing you think about before your operation."

These words were all Alex needed to hear. He had the best surgeon around and the anesthesiologist practically guaranteed a success. The medications he had received began to kick in and he felt somewhat lightheaded as images of events in his life began floating through his head in random order.

He remembered his dad taking him to the hospital on

weekends to make rounds, the fractured arm he suffered the first year at summer camp, his mother waiting for him after school the day her father died, and Annie on the night of her junior prom.

The visuals merged into one another as he fell deeper out of consciousness and although the conversations around him were still audible, they were barely intelligible. His eyes intermittently opened as he made contact with the various sets hovering over him as they peeked between the surgical caps and masks. One of his last visual memories was Dr. Addison's blue eyes and dark skin and the intensity he wore as the operation approached.

Then he saw Nicky. He imagined he was lying on an operating table next to him as the neurosurgeons worked on his tumor.

"It'll all be okay, Alex," he imagined Nicky saying, although he was not struggling for words on this occasion. "There's absolutely nothing to worry about. I have your rosary beads and you have my pendant and no one can hurt us. I'll be seeing you again, Alex; friends always meet again."

Although it was a drug-induced dream, it seemed real enough that it elevated Alex's blood pressure and forced the anesthesiologist to administer more sedatives. "This kid's not going down, David; I'll snow him a bit further."

The redosing put Alex under for good and he was completely anesthesized. Once asleep, the breathing tube was inserted into his trachea and taped to his cheeks. This was followed by the formal operative prep-during which he was doused in three layers of iodine solution from his neck to his thighs. His body was then covered in sterile drapes with the end result being a pile of blue cloth with a rectangular cutout of exposed skin overlying his breastbone.

Dr. Addison had left the room temporarily and returned after meticulously scrubbing his arms from fingertips to elbows. He approached the scrub tech with arms held above his waist and fingers pointing toward the sky. A towel was handed to him and he dried his upper extremities in a deliberate manner as he had done a thousand times before. A sterile blue gown was draped across his arms and he reflexively inserted his arms without poking his hands through. A second operating room technician quietly approached him from behind and tied the gown in a precise manner taking care not to contaminate the front. He eventually slipped his hands through the sleeves into a pair of flesh-tone latex gloves designed to protect the operator while being thin enough to provide maximum tactile discrimination. And so it went, day after day, the operating room ritual before each open-heart surgery. The movement of persons involved seemed completely choreographed and proceeded in silence like a ballet for the deaf.

Dr. Addison stepped up to the right side of the table and took a moment to remind himself that he was operating on the son of a very precious friend and colleague. He took a deep breath while grabbing the shiny scalpel and proceeded deliberately, taking care not to deviate from his routine despite the patient's V.I.P. status. The knife silently made contact with the skin as it went through dermis and the edges pulled slightly apart.

"Incision time 11:23," Dr. Billings announced as per standard protocol. The music was discontinued and all eyes were focused on the operative field. Dr. Addison used the electrocautery to get through subcutaneous tissues as he scored the sternum in the midline.

"Saw," he barked abruptly as the nurse handed him a sterile instrument resembling a jigsaw, "and drop the lungs."

The saw effortlessly cut through the child's breastbone as both sides pulled apart. A retractor aided in their separation as the sac around Alex's heart came into view.

"Looks a little full," the head surgeon announced to the room, commenting on how Alex's heart had enlarged pathologically with time. The sac was opened and the right heart protruded through as if it were relieved to have the overlying bone divided.

"Jesus Christ, look at the size of this ventricle. I'm not sure we're going to be able to do a simple repair here, ladies and germs." Dr. Addison's continuous comments made him seem like a ringmaster at a circus.

He proceeded to place sutures around the heart and eventually inserted the cannulas that would connect Alex to the heart-lung machine.

"Let's give the heparin, please."

The blood thinner was administered by the anesthesiologist in a metered fashion. This step was crucial in ensuring that Alex's blood would not clot the life-support system during the procedure as this complication was uniformly fatal.

"All right, lets go on."

This command set forth a flurry of activity as Turk and his crew drained the blood from Alex's body into their machine and eventually returned it through a separate circuit after it was oxygenated. The silence in the room was punctuated by the intermittent heartbeats from the anesthesiologist's monitors and the industrial hum of the perfusion pump.

"Cross-clamp, please, and Turk keep the mean pressure over fifty."

"Yes, sir, that's a can do."

"And what's with giving the kid a hard time Turk? I know he's a bit of a wise guy but he's just nervous. His dad was the same way; some of the funniest comments I've ever heard came from his father when one of our attendings was riding us during training."

"I'm sorry, sir, I thought the dude would appreciate the humor."

"Dude? Turk you've gotta stop acting like some reject from a damn cowboy ranch. I mean, this kid's life is being supported by your machine for the duration of this operation, can't you muster up some professionalism?"

"Yes, sir."

As the conversation dwindled, Dr. Addison applied the cross-clamp to Alex's aorta and initiated the delivery of a high-potassium cardioplegia solution.

"We have arrest, doctor," Turk commented as he noticed an absence of deflections on the overhead monitor. "I'll let you know at twenty minute intervals."

"That's great, Turk, and I'm putting in a sump to keep the ventricle decompressed."

As the heart arrested, Dr. Addison took a minute to reflect on the operation. He was repeatedly amazed by the technology that allowed him to safely stop an individual's heart, perform a corrective procedure, and have it resume activity. It was almost unnatural and in some societies, his patients would have been considered dead by all objective criteria during the operation.

"Every time I do this, I thank pioneers like Dr. Gibbons and his wife for giving us the ability to perform these wonderful operations. Man, Rufus, I can't tell you the rush I get when one of these babies goes just as planned and the patient is back on the playground in a couple of weeks."

Rufus had heard this dissertation before and responded supportively in an instinctive fashion. These moments of reflection and surgeon-stroking had become a part of his job description and went by almost unnoticed. Dr. Addison continued to divide the sac around Alex's heart and directly visualized the enlarged right side and abnormal anatomy.

"Guys, I don't think we're gonna be able to perform a Bastelli repair here. I'm concerned about the right ventricular outflow tract. Turk, call my office before we go on pump and let Jennie know that I may need her to thaw one of the bovine jugulars."

Although this cryptic message would be unintelligible to the layperson, Turk knew exactly what he meant and was practically on the phone before Dr. Addison had finished his sentence.

"Any particular size?"

"Give me a couple of minutes, I'm not there yet."

Dr. Addison meticulously dissected Alex's heart and began the reparative process. Through the upper chamber on the right side he was able to visualize the hole and expeditiously patched it with a synthetic cloth derivative.

Intermittently the heart tried to beat as it warmed and the cardioplegia solution became ineffective but redosing put the organ in its temporary hibernating state.

He continued his reconstruction of the right heart all the while wondering if it would be successful. When he was finished, two and a half hours had lapsed on the heart-lung machine.

"All right folks, let's try and come off," he said, indicating he was ready to wean Alex from the heart-lung machine. "And I want to run some background nitric oxide, okay?"

Dr. Billings knew that this was his cue to initiate the inhalation agent and he did so promptly. "All set, David, let's give the kid a crack at coming off."

Dr. Addison initiated the weaning process. "Drop your flows and fill him up a little bit, Turk. His ventricle seems like it's struggling a little bit so turn up the inotropes and give him some volume, Billings."

Upon hearing this, Dr. Billings rapidly infused five hundred milliliters of saline solution through a large-bore IV placed in Alex's neck. As he peered over the drapes and inspected Alex's heart, he commented, "Jesus, Dave, I've fed better pieces of meat to my dogs."

This casual reference to Alex's current heart appearance irritated Dr. Addison and he curtly responded, "Listen,

Billings, if I want your unsolicited advice I'll call your secretary and we'll do lunch, okay? In the meantime, keep your asinine comments to yourself and just do your job."

The tension in the room could have been cut with a scalpel and the tone of Dr. Addison's voice proved disconcerting to those in the operating room as he was rarely flappable; he was obviously concerned about the potential outcome and realizing Alex was the son of a good friend made the situation exponentially worse.

"Turk, keep droppin' your flows and try to come off."

As the heart-lung machine decreased its contribution to supporting Alex's circulation his hemodynamics became worse. The heart became distended and eventually a rhythm change prompted the reinstitution of bypass.

"God damn it," Dr. Addison exclaimed. "This case is giving me a rash. We're screwed; this heart has absolutely no intention of working independently and we're already three hours in the hole." This last statement was made in reference to the time spent on pump, as it was approaching a dangerous level. "I'm scrubbing out to talk to Mark. Go back on full bypass and support him till I get back."

With this, he violently removed his gown and flung his gloves across the room. His pace quickened as he stormed out of the operative suite but the others ignored the tirade. Meanwhile, Alex's heart remained dormant and his life was completely supported by the expensive piece of machinery under the direction of Turk in room ten.

The OR waiting room was surprisingly cold compared to the rest of the hospital, and was full of expectant parents as they agonized over their children's plights. Mr. and Mrs. Harkins had assumed a position in the corner of the room between a free coffee machine and television set. They had been commiserating with Mrs. Malhotra during the morning's ordeal and sharing stories of both youngsters as children. An arrangement had been made for Alex to visit Nicky in late August and this was the surprise his father had promised upon returning to Mills Creek.

Dr. Addison entered the room and began searching for Alex's parents. His father was the first to notice the entrance and was surprised by the rapidity in which the operation had been performed. His excitement turned to worry almost immediately as he saw the expression on his colleague's face. He knew exactly what was happening as he, himself, had made this visit with adult patients.

"Everything okay, David? Did he come off all right?" The question caught his wife's attention and she jumped out of her seat toward Dr. Addison. Anxiety overcame her as she sensed the frustration of her son's surgeon.

"Oh my god. Can we see him yet Dr. Addison? Is he doing okay? Did the procedure go well?"

"Why don't you folks have a seat," Dr. Addison said as he found one for himself, "and let me catch you up." The parents sat down and held each other's hand until they blanched. They had convinced themselves they were prepared for the worst but now reality was setting in, as was a state of disbelief.

"It's like this, Mark. Alex's right heart is pretty shot. I tried an annular patch and pulmonary augmentation but it's just not going to work. He's spent three hours on the pump and his myocardium's definitely a bit stunned. I have to re-create his outflow tract and we don't have a homograft in his size and, unfortunately, he's too big for a monocusp reconstruction."

The conversation took on a very technical tone and was well above the head of Alex's mother. She could, however, decipher that things weren't going well and Dr. Addison was running out of tricks.

"I could put in a bovine jugular vein as an outflow tract. It hasn't been approved by the Food and Drug Administration, but I've placed several of them in children at the Stadt Hospital in Heidelberg earlier this year. I'm going to have to get a stat compassionate use approval from the hospital's administration and we'll have to deal with the FDA later. It's going to mean at least another two hours on the pump, though."

"David," Alex's father began, "I entrusted you with my oldest son for a reason. You're the best pediatric heart surgeon around and I have complete confidence in you. You go ahead and do whatever you think is best and get him off that pump and back to Maine."

The pressure of the situation was enormous and Dr. Addison had hoped that at least Mark would've understood the gravity of the situation. He couldn't guarantee a success and wanted the parents to stay realistic; he wasn't sure he could get Alex back to Maine.

"If things don't work out, David, I'll still know that he got the best care possible."

Alex's father realized that he had placed added pressure on his friend with his last comment and felt obligated to redirect the conversation. This was an effective move as a sense of relief instantly came over Dr. Addison's face as he stood to return to the operating room.

"I'll call the administrators from the OR and proceed with the jugular vein. See you in a couple of hours."

Alex's mother had been speechless throughout the entire exchange and felt as if she were in a dream. Were they really talking about her son not making it? He had a whole family waiting for him back home and a trip to New York planned for the summer. What was going on?

The look of despair on her face escaped no one and she felt her husband's arms around her in an embrace.

"Don't worry, baby. I've seen David operate, and I don't

 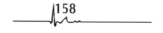

mean with the nurses. He's the best."

Sometimes a little levity can diffuse a potentially tense situation but this was not one of those occasions. The parents sat back down and the rest of the wait would be spent in silence as both individuals reminisced about times spent with Alex. Mrs. Malhotra had been knitting feverishly next to them as she, too, had been reminiscing. This activity was an excellent distraction from the day's events. She was making a cap Nicky could wear after the operation as the surgery required that his head be shaved.

Dr. Addison returned to the operating room and received an update regarding Alex's vitals. As he replaced his surgical loupes and operative headlight, he began barking a series of orders.

"I want Ken McAffey on the line. We're going with a bovine jugular. I know this team hasn't put one in before so I'll need a couple of 4-0 proline sutures, some big pledgets, a new left atrial line, and some thrombin gelfoam. Let's move it folks; the longer we spend on pump, the less likely he'll come off."

He exited the room to scrub and the OR personnel jumped into action in order to retrieve the items needed. As the nurses were gowning him, Ken McAffey returned his call. "Put him on speaker phone. Ken, can you hear me? It's David."

"Go ahead; I can hear you fine."

"We've got a bit of a situation here. Remember those bovine jugulars I put in over in Germany? Well, I need to put one of those puppies into this little boy on the table."

"You know those aren't approved by the FDA, don't you?"

"Jesus Christ, Kenny, quit being such a god damn administrator for once in your life. I'm talking about a little boy here, for god's sake."

"Well, Dave, I'll have to convene a meeting of the hospital's policy board and then it will have to be approved by the ethics committee. Let me get working on that."

"You know what, Ken, next time you actually enter the hospital why don't you peek into an operating room so you can see what the hell is going on in here since you're making all the decisions for the patients instead of us doctors. This kid's been on pump for almost three and a half hours and I'll need another two to get the damn thing in. I don't have time for all your hospital mumbo jumbo and neither does this kid. I'm putting it in and you can fire me later if you want to. I've got to go now."

McAffey realized that losing Dr. Addison would be a huge blow to the program and firing him would need an act of God. "All right, David, you push on and we'll deal with the FDA later. Good luck."

"Thanks, Ken."

Dr. Addison felt badly about being so abrupt but he was getting sick of the hospital politics, and to him patients always came first. As the conversation ended, his assistant entered the room with the implant as it had been thawing since the initial phone call.

The surgeon proceeded efficiently as he excised a large portion of Alex's heart and replaced it with the cow's vein. It looked beautiful when completed, although the total pump time was now over five hours. As the final stitches were placed, he asked the perfusionists to rewarm the patient. The cross-clamp was released and the cardioplegia solution which had maintained arrest during the procedure was washed out of the heart and activity resumed. With time, the rhythm became more regular and the heart function visibly improved.

"All right, Turk, let's give it another go. Fill him up a little bit and drop your flows." On this occasion, the heart looked substantially better and despite the precariously long pump run, it seemed Alex may come off.

"C'mon, baby, come to papa," Dr. Addison said, as if talking directly to the heart may provide it extra motivation. "We're looking pretty good here, folks. Slide off, Turk, and let's see what the boy can do on his own."

With that, cardiopulmonary bypass was terminated and the responsibility for circulating blood to the body and the lungs now lay on Alex and the small section of a cow that was part of his heart. Fortunately, the vital signs continued to improve and his heart was functioning beautifully. Dr. Addison let out a sigh of relief as he temporarily stepped back from the table.

"Nice job, doctor."

"Thanks, everybody. You've all been great. Let's dry up in the chest a little more and then begin closing. Send for my last case." The whole process was about to begin again.

Dr. Addison scrubbed out at the terminal portion of the operation as his assistants closed the skin. This time he had a smile on his face as he approached the waiting area and this didn't go beyond the notice of Alex's parents.

"The heart looks pretty good, folks. They're closing right now and he'll be in the PICU within a half hour. You can see him then. We still have to worry about his head a little since he was on support for so long but he's young and healthy and I think he'll have a full recovery."

"Thank you so much, Dr. Addison. Thanks for saving our little boy. We both knew you'd do it all along." It appeared the cat had returned the tongue to Alex's mother.

After Alex's chest was closed, he was transported to the pediatric intensive care unit. A period of rewarming followed and eventually his family was allowed to visit. His father made several phone calls back home to update the rest of the family before sitting at his bedside.

"He looks so peaceful, doesn't he?" his father said staring at Alex's swollen face. "It'll take a couple of days for him to mobilize the fluid he's received and stop looking like the Michelin man."

"I'm so glad he's okay, Mark. I thought I was going to die when I saw Dr. Addison the first time. It sounds like he had to get a little bit creative to get our Alex off the table, doesn't it?"

"You bet; but that's why I chose him."

The remainder of the evening was relatively uneventful for the Harkins family as Alex recovered from his operation. His parents sat by his bedside until visiting hours were over and Dr. Addison saw him for a final time after the completion of his last case.

"Looks like the chest tube drainage is reasonable for such a monster pump run," he commented to the nurse taking care of him for the evening. "Just keep an eye on his blood gases and let me know if he so much as flinches from a hemodynamic standpoint. And another thing, don't give him any sedation as I want to evaluate him neurologically as soon as possible."

"Yes, Dr. Addison. His parents left a message for you to call them at the inn at your earliest convenience."

"Thank you. I'll give them a ring from the car on my drive home. Please keep his mean pressures slightly elevated so he perfuses his brain until everything settles out."

The next morning was a haze for Alex. As the anesthesia wore off, he found himself coming in and out of consciousness. The boundaries between reality and a dream state seemed obscured and he remained under the effects of a paralytic agent administered by the anesthesiologist. Eventually the fast-twitch muscles became effective and he was able to open his eyes. His first recollection of the awakening process would be of a beautiful nurse tending to him gingerly as she adminstered saline drops into his eyes and wiped the saliva from his chin as it accumulated around the endotracheal tube.

He did feel somewhat trapped within his body as the ability to move escaped him due to the medications. The ICU personnel directed a barrage of questions in his direction regarding his status and he was unable to answer them for the time being.

Throughout the morning his stream of consciousness varied and eventually he was able to process his surroundings. Surprisingly, once his senses had returned, he saw Nicky at his bedside. His head was wrapped circumferentially in a sterile white dressing and he stood adjacent to an IV pole supporting several drips.

"Man, Alex, you look like crap," Nicky uttered as the words were freely flowing for the first time. "Could you possibly have any more fluid in your face?"

Alex tried to respond but couldn't with the breathing tube in his throat. In his excitement, his heart rate increased prompting the nurse to enter the room and administer an agent to slow it.

"Relax, Alex, everything's going just fine. Your heart is squeezing beautifully. Just try and calm down and before you know it, we'll get you off the ventilator."

Alex tried to motion toward Nicky but was unsuccessful.

Nicky continued, "Man, Alex, they had a rough time with my operation but it turned out okay. I'm a little bit sore but I'm speaking better and my right arm's comin' back. I can't wait until that plastic cigar you're smoking comes out and we can talk again. I've got a lot to tell you about Manhattan when everything's said and done."

Alex wished desperately to respond but was unable to do so. He wanted to tell Nicky how glad he was that the operation went fine for both of them and how surprised he was that Nicky had recovered so quickly. He just couldn't speak with the breathing tube in and was probably too tired to communicate anyway. Eventually fatigue got the better of him and he drifted back to sleep.

The remainder of the day was spent in a deep slumber. His chest tube drainage was minimal and they were removed on the morning of the second postoperative day. Finally the anesthetic and paralytic agents wore off and he was able to remain awake to the point that the ventilator was no longer necessary. His parents sat diligently at his bedside and although they seemed happy, their expressions contained a hint of concern bordering on worry.

After the tube was removed he tried to talk but found it somewhat difficult given the swelling of his vocal cords. "Did . . . did every . . . did everything go okay?"

"You bet, son," his father responded with great enthusiasm. "Your heart's great for another one hundred thousand miles although the warranty is only good for seven years or seventy thousand, whichever comes first."

Alex was able to muster a smile although even this activity seemed to take a fair amount of effort.

"Thirsty," he said, sounding like an immigrant who had recently moved to the country and was unable to formulate complete sentences. "Need water."

His mother supported a Styrofoam cup and straw under his chin as Alex sipped tentatively. Nurse Renee entered the room and would be taking care of him for the next shift.

"Geez, Alex, you must be some kind of VIP or something. We've got the queen bee taking care of you today."

Alex's dad and Nurse Renee did have a bit of a history dating back to his training days and their initial meeting was somewhat uncomfortable. They struggled in deciding between a handshake or hug as the initial greeting and eventually settled on a peck on the cheek.

"Honey, this is Renee, one of the best nurses in Dodge and this is my wife Jane, also a nurse but more recently the perennial winner of mother of the year." This title was obviously a fragment of his father's imagination but the sentence was effective in immediately communicating his father's commitment to the family and that his nurse-chasing days were over.

"Pleasure to meet you," both women responded in unison.

"Well it seems like Alex is doing great," Renee informed them, "and he'll probably spend most of the day sleeping." This description was right on the money as Alex did doze off frequently during the next twenty-four hours. His weariness preempted him from inquiring about his friend Nicky although he was very much in the back of Alex's mind.

The third morning was like an awakening; Alex felt absolutely wonderful. He awoke with newfound energy to find that all but one of his intravenous lines and heart catheters had been removed. With assistance he sat up in a chair before his parents' arrival and gave them the most pleasant of surprises.

"Well look at you, will ya? Man, Alex, you look like a million bucks! I can't believe you're making such rapid progress."

"I feel great, Mom, like I could run a marathon."

"Yeah, and you won't be turning blue at the end anymore, right, son?"

"You bet, Dad. Let's get rid of that motorized bike when we get home and get me a ten-speed like the one you have. I'll be able to race you into town in no time."

"Done."

The rest of the morning was spent making plans for Alex's transfer to the floor and eventually home. The trio laughed and hugged while making special efforts to thank all the health-care personnel involved in Alex's care.

"Hey, where's Nicky? He hasn't visited in a couple of days. Is he still in the ICU or did he get transferred out already?"

Both parents directed their gazes to the ground as they were afraid to maintain eye contact with Alex lest their secret be discovered.

"What the heck's going on here? You both look like you've seen a ghost and it couldn't possibly be me because my oxygen saturations are reading ninety-eight percent, according to that monitor. All I want to know is why Nicky hasn't visited."

"Alex, we were going to tell you after a few more days of recovery and I still think that's a good idea."

"Dad, what are you talking about?" He sensed that something was wrong and needed to know the truth. "What aren't you guys tellin' me? Nicky's okay, isn't he? I mean he looked great a couple of days ago." Neither parent understood Alex's comment.

"I don't know what you're talking about, but you might as well hear the story. I think you're strong enough." His father waited for a nod in the affirmative from his mother before continuing. "Nicky had a very long and difficult operation the same day as yours which, in fact, took almost twenty hours. His doctors encountered a fair amount of bleeding during the procedure and the cancer was unresectable. Since the operation, Nicky has been in a coma and they don't think he's going to come out of it. Even if he does, they're worried about his level of function given the amount he bled into his brain and the invasiveness of the cancer. Overall, the prognosis is pretty poor."

Alex couldn't believe what he was hearing. What was his dad talking about? Alex had seen Nicky with his own eyes a couple of days ago and he looked great. Obviously his parents were misinformed.

"That can't possibly be true. I mean, I just saw the guy and all he had was a little bandage on his head. He came into my room under his own power and his speech and right arm were much better."

"Son, you were still under the influence of the anesthetic

at that point and probably dreamed the encounter. Nicky hasn't moved since the day of surgery and hasn't been able to breathe over the ventilator."

"You mean he's going to be a vegetable the rest of his life?"

"It's quite possible, son. Your mother and I have been sick to our stomachs over this and are even more grateful that your operation was so successful. Mrs. Malhotra, on the other hand, looks like she is half dead but fortunately her family has flown out to join her."

Alex just couldn't fathom what had happened. Nicky had said that he was going to be fine before the operation and Alex could sense the same thing. This was terrible. As the facts settled in, he realized that the conversation the boys had probably was not real. He began to cry uncontrollably and his parents tried to rally around him but the eleven year old was inconsolable.

He eventually gathered himself and declared that he wished to visit his friend. "I'm not sure that's such a great idea, Alex. Remember, you're still recovering from open-heart surgery." The boy was insistent and his parents eventually acquiesced against their better judgment. Alex was too feeble to make the trek down the hall under his own power; therefore, his family requested a wheelchair.

As the Harkins family approached room four, they passed several of Nicky's relatives as they left the grieving parents. An elderly female, perhaps Nicky's other grandmother, was also in a wheelchair and had her head buried in her hands as she left Nicky's room.

"Dad, is there anything we can do to help these people? They look miserable."

"I don't think so, Alex, but I'll approach Mrs. Malhotra when the time is appropriate and lend our support. This is an extremely unfortunate situation and I think they've handled it pretty graciously to this point. Son, are you sure you're up to this right now?"

"Yeah, Dad, please wheel me over." The incongruity of the situation became painfully obvious to Alex as it unfolded and he was more grateful than ever for Dr. Addison's skills and his speedy recovery from surgery.

Upon approaching room four, he peered around the corner and saw Mrs. Malhotra at Nicky's bedside, his hand clenched in hers. She kept mumbling something that was unintelligible to him as he entered the room.

"Meri beta, Meri piari beta," she repeated as she buried her head into his bed hoping he would wake up and make spontaneous movements. "Please, Nikou, please wake up."

The sight of a grown woman grieving took Alex by complete surprise and was somewhat intimidating. The monitors provided some background noise as the rest of the relatives remained in silence catering to the grieving mother.

Alex didn't know if his visit would be welcomed or serve as a painful reminder to Mrs. Malhotra of the son she was about to lose. He asked to be wheeled next to her but did not initiate a conversation until spoken to.

"Hello, Alex," Mrs. Malhotra said without raising her head. "I thank you for coming here. My little Nickou thought about you as he was falling asleep before surgery according to the anesthesiologists and I'm glad you're here now. I can't express how happy I am that your heart is fixed and that you're feeling well. I wish Nikhil could tell you that himself. I can't describe to you what I'm feeling right now but, for whatever reason, I feel much more comfortable with you in the room. It's like Nicky is here himself."

"Mrs. Malhotra, I don't necessarily understand what's going on, but he looked great to me a couple of days ago."

"What are you talking about, Alex?"

Alex reminded himself he was referring to a conversation that obviously didn't occur and made an immediate effort to modify his statement. "Nothing, Mrs. Malhotra. I'm so sorry his operation wasn't a complete success."

"Yes, we all wished that it turned out differently, but life's a bit unpredictable. I would give anything to hear Nicky's voice right now and I wouldn't care if he stuttered or struggled to have a conversation. Alex, I've spent the last three days thinking I'll never hear the sound of his voice again."

Mrs. Malhotra's grave tone was eye opening for Alex as he began to realize the finality of the circumstances. His friend was really sick and was probably going to die. Their summer together in Manhattan would never happen.

"You can't give up the ship here, ma'am; I'm pretty sure he'll come around."

"Alex, do you remember the little boy, David, in your room before the operation? Do you remember how it seemed that life had been sucked out of him?"

"I remember David, Mrs. Malhotra."

"Nicky made me promise to never leave him like that. His doctors think his chances of recovery are impossible given the tumor and all the bleeding, and under the best of circumstances he wouldn't see his thirteenth birthday."

"But at least you can spend some time with him like this."

"My dear Alex, at some point everyone has to make a decision about the *quality* of life versus the *quantity* of life. I've had long discussions with all his brothers and sisters as well as my husband. We want to remember little Nickou the way he was. We want to remember the intelligent little boy who brought joy and happiness to our lives every day and taught us the meaning of unselfishness. His biggest worry going into this operation was how he'd be disrupting our lives."

"What about the rest of us who just started to get to know

him? I mean, we just became friends and had these huge operations together. We'll never get to play again."

"Friends always meet again, Alex. Nicky will enter your life in some capacity in the future; you can count on it. You may see him in a stranger's eyes or in a new friend you make in school, but I guarantee you that your friendship is not over."

"I don't know what to say."

"Don't say anything. Come join us in a puja."

Alex came to learn that a puja was a joint prayer the Hindus held on special occasions. Eleven of Nicky's relatives had gathered at the bedside as the nurses had allowed more visitors than usual given the circumstances. The curtains were drawn and Nicky's father began the prayer.

"Oh Bagwan, thank you for allowing Nicky to enter our lives. None of us understand why you would take such a precious flower from us after a few short years but we have to defer to your judgment and assume this is a part of your master plan. He has enriched our lives in the short time with us and will occupy a small place in our hearts as we move on and try to continue life without him. I will miss him every day. I will miss taking him to school. I will miss his face across from mine at the dinner table; and I will miss kissing his soft face good night each night. I will turn the anger I am feeling right now into something productive and feed it into the perpetual circle of our lives. Seera, would you like to add anything?"

"Yes, Vinod, I would. I would like to thank Bagwan for making Alex's recovery so expeditious and his operation a success. I, too, do not understand why our family was graced by such a beautiful child for such a short time but I am grateful to have known Nicky and will have him in my soul for the rest of my life. I thank you, Bhagwan, for the eleven wonderful years that Nicky spent with us."

Alex was awash with emotion and he couldn't believe what he was hearing. Why weren't these people breaking things in anger and yelling at the top of their lungs? They had just lost someone very dear to them and they were acting as if someone had done them a favor. What the hell were they thinking?

Nicky's relatives beginning chanting a Hindu mantra slowly in unison as his father swept a ceremonial cloth over his forehead. His mother proceeded to take the article of clothing and symbolically draped it over his face as if she had shut his eyes guaranteeing eternal rest. Each family member then knelt by his bedside taking turns holding his warm but lifeless hands as they wished him farewell and asked him to return to their lives at a later time. The process continued for almost three hours as moments of silence were interrupted by joint prayer. Alex didn't understand the language but the message was universal, as was the grieving process. Alex's parents had been watching the proceedings from outside the room and were eventually invited in by Nikhil's father.

"Come, let us give thanks for your son as we grieve our own misfortune."

Alex's parents assumed a kneeling position next to Alex's wheelchair and offered their own prayer in silence. Mrs. Malhotra was overcome by the ceremony and began wailing in a tone that could only be achieved by a grieving mother. She fell on the floor next to her youngest son and her high-pitched shrieks were punctuated intermittently by the sounds of Nicky's ventilator and infusion pumps.

"Meri beta, Meri chota beta," she kept repeating incessantly in Hindi. Her son was in her hands but he was no longer alive.

Eventually Nicky's father pulled Mrs. Malhotra to her feet and stated, "It is time." She hesitantly nodded as she covered her head in a shawl and stared at the ground. The remaining family members left the room in single file like a jury entering a courtroom. Alex's father began to wheel him away when he blankly stated, "I'm staying; he would want me to stay."

His parents exchanged glances and Mrs. Malhotra raised her head and established eye contact long enough for them to understand that this would be acceptable. The remaining party consisted of Alex, Mr. and Mrs. Malhotra, two of their children, and Nikhil.

Renee entered the room and drew the curtain behind her. She had been administering boluses of morphine to Nicky for the last twenty-four hours to keep him as comfortable and pain-free as possible. On this occasion, she had ten milligrams, twice the usual dose, as she anticipated the end.

"Are you all comfortable with this decision," she asked half hoping that someone would say "no".

After a long pause, Mrs. Malhotra shook her head as only her sunken eyes could be seen around the shawl. The entire syringe was injected in a peripheral vein and this was followed by a saline flush to ensure that the drug would circulate. Renee proceeded to turn off the overhead monitor before disconnecting the tip of Nicky's endotracheal tube from the coiled tubing attached to the ventilator. Nicky would be breathing on his own for the final time.

Mrs. Malhotra wept quietly trying to maintain dignity for her son's benefit. Nicky's siblings could no longer stand the final act and excused themselves, as did his father.

Nicky lay in bed looking comfortable and his breathing was still audible. The interval between each exhalation became longer and Alex stared at his chest as it rose and fell. Every pause seemed like it would be the final one, but he secretly rejoiced each time Nicky initiated a spontaneous breath. He kept thinking this was a bad dream and Nicky would jump out of bed and take credit for this ultimate practical joke.

All at once Nicky began flailing his arms and partially sat up in bed.

"He's not ready to die, Mrs. Malhotra; he's fighting it. Please put him back on the ventilator. We're killing him! Just look at him; he's moving." Alex's voice was shrill as he felt like an accomplice to the most heinous of crimes. "We can't just do nothing. Nurse, please come back and put him on the breathing machine."

Mrs. Malhotra grabbed Alex in a firm embrace and although he initially tried to break free, her persistence and his sense of futility allowed him to bury his head in her arms quietly.

"It's okay, Alex; it's just a reflex. His doctor warned me that this is not uncommon after a brain injury. Nicky is gone, Alex. Let him live in your memory. He is gone."

After some time Alex raised his eyes to inspect his bedridden friend. There were no more movements; his chest didn't rise; and his color had turned gray. Alex wheeled himself next to the bedrail just close enough to touch Nicky's hand. It felt cold and dry, as he imagined it would. Nicky was dead.

Alex sat back in his wheelchair and took in a deep breath trying to process the events as they had developed. All of a sudden the seriousness of the moment became overwhelming and he felt suffocated. Instinctively, he wheeled his chair toward the door anticipating an unnoticed departure. In the meantime, Mrs. Malhotra had assumed a position next to Nicky's bed laying her head next to his as mother and son shared a pillow for the final time. She let his cold and bloodless cheek caress hers as her eyes closed, imagining he was still alive.

Nicky's dad sat upon the window ledge as it overlooked

a small playground within the confines of the hospital. Small children occupied the swings and played as if nothing had happened and, in reality, Nicky's death did not affect them at all. The newspaper truck drove into the circular drive approaching the hospital as its driver mouthed a song on the radio. The hospital security guard was making small talk with the parking attendant as they flipped through the sports section of the newspaper. Visitors were coming and going as if nothing happened. "Don't they know Nickou's dead," he whispered, intending the comment for himself.

Alex awkwardly backed into the glass dividers as he tried to make a clean escape and this caught the attention of both parents in the room. He looked back and forth at them as he silently asked permission to retire temporarily from the grieving process. Mrs. Malhotra's eyes were sunken and underlined by large black circles and they approved of Alex's departure, realizing that he was still recovering from his own trauma.

His parents were waiting for him outside the room and each was fighting back tears. What a poignant moment this was and they felt somewhat guilty for feeling relief and joy for their son's success while this other family suffered such a loss.

"Let's head back to the room, son; I wish you didn't have to see that."

"I wanted to see that, Dad. I'm glad you filled me in before it was too late."

Upon returning to his own room, Alex carefully transferred himself from the wheelchair to the bed taking care to pamper his breastbone lest it dehisce while healing. He covered himself up to his eyes with a blanket and stared at the blank screen of the television monitor.

"Well I think you'll be transferred to the floor tomorrow, honey, and Dr. Addison indicated that you may be discharged in a few days. Annie and Molly have been calling for you three times a day and perhaps you can return the favor when you feel up to it. They say Sandy Cromwell's been stopping by the house each day and seems quite concerned for your welfare. I didn't realize that you both were so close."

"I like Sandy, Mom. I'll call the girls this evening."

"How about a quick game of travel chess?" his father offered, desperate for a distraction.

"I don't think so, Dad. In fact, I'd like to be alone for a while if it's okay with you guys."

"Are you sure, honey?"

"I'm positive, Mom; I've got a lot to think about."

Alex hadn't known Nicky very long but liked everything he represented. A young boy with an inexplicable illness had fought the odds and found a way to enjoy life until the end. He remained unselfish and caring despite the knowledge that his cancer would most likely be fatal. Both boys' situations weren't completely dissimilar except that Alex would be going home in a few days and Nicki would be cremated. The whole situation was sickening.

The next morning Alex was transferred to his previous room on the fourth floor. The nurses made a fuss over his return, which included a small party at Camp Ridgewood with the other postoperative children. David remained in a coma attached to his ventilator in the corner of the room. The Ahmeds had been discharged and had been replaced by another child, with another illness, whose parents were steadfast in keeping him company during the hospitalization.

At any hour, children could be seen packing and unpacking their bags as they entered and were discharged from Ridgewood Children's Hospital. Fear could be seen in children of all ages-fear of the unknown, fear of the pain they were required to endure, fear of dying.

Alex had met with the Malhotras on the day prior to his own discharge and they insisted that the invitation to visit Manhattan was still valid. He gracefully accepted and felt a need to spend time with this family for unexplainable reasons.

"I see Nicky in you, Alex," Mrs. Malhotra stated as goodbyes were being exchanged.

"I wish I could say the same," he replied.

"Don't worry, Alex; you will see him again. Perhaps in

another person, or an animal, maybe even yourself."

Alex felt as if he'd aged twenty years in the last few days; he had lived through open-heart surgery and witnessed his first death all within a seventy-two-hour span. He was ready to return home to spend time with family, those individuals who were kind enough to keep him in their thoughts and see him through this ordeal.

The taxicab pulled up to the entrance of the hospital and the driver predictably rolled up onto the sidewalk. Alex's parents loaded their bags into the trunk as he was assisted into the rear seat.

As the engine started, Dr. French pulled up next to them in his convertible.

"Hey, Alex, I promised you a ride. Did you forget?

"Oh, thank you, Dr. French, but I'm not really feeling up to it at the moment. Perhaps in a few months after my post-operative check."

"Suit yourself, young man, and take care of yourself."

The truth of the matter was that the whole idea just didn't seem that appealing to Alex anymore. Sports cars were fine, but they weren't Annie, Molly, or his grandparents. He longed to be in their company and had resigned to inform them how much he had missed them the last few days. He looked forward to visiting Mr. McKinley and Sister Agatha and riding his bicycle with his father into town. These activities would no longer be taken for granted as he came to realize the importance of family, friends, and the simple pleasures of life.

The cab headed through town toward the international airport and a Northeast Airlines flight that would soon be transporting the Harkins family back to Maine. He thanked God for his new heart and for helping him see the beauty in his life. Ridgewood Hospital disappeared in the back window. He was going home.